FORT

A woman wa[s] center of the da[rk]
"Do come in," Xaviera, the cla[ir]

I moved closer ...... across from her. "You are here to celebrate your birthday, to learn the future," Xaviera said encouragingly. Suddenly she dropped her hands to the table and gazed into the crystal ball with intensity.

"What do you see?" I croaked.

She raised her eyes to meet mine. "I see a challenging summer ahead for you. And there is an overwhelming aura of love surrounding you," she continued. "A young man very near us—certainly on the premises—loves you very deeply. But I do not see his face. Perhaps you already know who it is." She watched me expectantly.

"Uh, no," I admitted sheepishly. "I—I'm unattached right now."

"Then keep your eyes and ears open," she said. "There will surely be signs."

"Because you see signs?" I asked. My heart was pounding.

"No." Xaviera smiled for the first time. "Because I know teenage boys."

Bantam Sweet Dreams Romances
Ask your bookseller for the books you have missed

Fortunes of Love

Mary Schultz

BANTAM BOOKS

TORONTO • NEW YORK • LONDON • SYDNEY • AUCKLAND

RL 6, IL age 11 and up

FORTUNES OF LOVE
A Bantam Book/December 1989

*Sweet Dreams and its associated logo are registered
trademarks of Bantam Books. a division of Bantam
Doubleday Dell Publishing Group, Inc. Registered in
U.S. Patent and Trademark Office and elsewhere.*

Cover photo by Pat Hill.

ISBN 0-553-27358-2

Published simultaneously in the United States and Canada

*Bantam Books are published by Bantam Books, a division of
Bantam Doubleday Dell Publishing Group, Inc. Its trademark,
consisting of the words "Bantam Books" and the portrayal of a
rooster, is Registered in U.S. Patent and Trademark Office and
in other countries. Marca Registrada. Bantam Books, Inc., 666 Fifth
Avenue, New York, New York 10103.*

Printed and bound in Great Britain by
Cox & Wyman Ltd., Reading

Fortunes of Love

Chapter One

"So it's true, Karen Daly!"

My best friend Mandy Bennett marched through my bedroom doorway, her round face set in determined lines.

"Mandy, what—"

"Peter was right," she interrupted. "You really are still up here in your room, lying flat on your bed, staring up at the ceiling."

"For your information, there are very interesting cracks right around the light fixture," I told her. I sat up and swung my legs over the edge of the bed.

"And you're still in your bathrobe," Mandy chided, pointing an accusing finger at me.

"I've been doing some serious thinking," I explained with a sigh. "Guess I lost track of the time."

"This is no time to think, Karen. Your birth-

1

day party is going to start in half an hour." Mandy sat beside me on the bed and put a friendly arm around my shoulders.

"Sweet sixteen and no one to kiss," I said forlornly.

"I think the saying goes, 'sweet sixteen and *never* been kissed.' And we both know that doesn't apply to you! You went steady with Jeremy during our entire sophomore year. He kissed you lots of times." Mandy smiled knowingly.

"Well, I've never needed a date more than I do today," I said. "I have to attend my own party without a guy."

"I could understand your being bummed if Jeremy had been the one to dump you, but you let him go, remember?"

Did I ever remember! Telling him I wanted my freedom had been awful. We'd argued for two solid hours in the parking lot at Romano's Pizza Nook. Jeremy had wanted me to shut everybody out of my life but him, and I just hadn't been able to go along with it anymore. I had been feeling stifled. I needed my own space. "Even though things weren't working out, I suppose breaking up with Jeremy two weeks before my birthday wasn't very practical."

"It had to be done," Mandy said sagely.

"Yeah, I guess so," I said with resignation. "But adjusting to being alone again is tougher than I expected."

2

"You're moping around as though your dating days are over!" Mandy said with a scoff. "Not all boys expect you to give them a hundred percent of your time. You just have to let everybody know you're in circulation again."

I walked over to my dresser and gazed into my makeup mirror. My sun-bleached brown hair looked pretty good since I'd had trimmed the uneven ends. My green eyes still had some sparkle to them, even though I'd been crying a lot lately. And everybody said I had great legs, long and lean. I guessed boys might find me attractive . . .

"You don't think Jeremy will show up at the party, do you?" I asked, biting my lower lip nervously.

"He wouldn't dare!" Mandy gasped. "You didn't invite him, so I'm sure he knows better."

I opened my makeup case and began to apply plum eyeshadow on my lids so my eyes would look greener. "I hope this summer isn't going to be a total fizzle for both of us."

"Give it a chance, Karen," Mandy said, coaxingly. "It's only June twenty-seventh." Then she added with a giggle. "We've only begun to fight—uh, flirt."

"Yeah, right," I agreed, running some bright red lipstick along my lips. "Do you think this color is too much?" I turned to Mandy, who was still sitting on my bed.

"Hey, you turned sixteen today, remember? You're old enough to know what's best for you."

"Somehow I don't feel any wiser," I admitted.

"In that case, it clashes with the eyeshadow."

"Great," I groaned. "I can't even handle lipstick, much less the rest of my life."

"Yes, you can! And you have so much going for you—like a family who cares enough to throw you a great party." Mandy took my arm and pulled me over to the window. "Just look at all the Dalys down there," she said, gesturing to the backyard two stories below. "Not every girl gets to celebrate her sixteenth birthday with a miniature carnival."

I gazed down at the rectangle of lawn enclosed by a chain-link fence. All the members of my family were busily preparing for my party in the warm Saturday afternoon sunshine. My brother Peter was testing a giant ring toss game he had constructed with the help of a *Popular Mechanics* article. My older sister Tiffany was arranging a makeshift stage for her amateur magic act. My younger sister Joy was standing in our white gazebo in her hula skirt and red plastic lei, wiggling her pudgy legs and singing a Hawaiian song she had learned in dance class.

"Look at Joy down there practicing her big

4

number," Mandy said. "Now *that's* entertainment."

"The very best," I agreed with a wide smile. I had the feeling that this party-carnival was going to be my best birthday ever. I turned my attention to my mother, who was securing a vinyl cloth to our redwood picnic table, then to my father, who was firing up his barbecue for the hamburgers and hot dogs. They were all working together to make my party happen. My family had always loved occasions to celebrate, and it touched me to know they were going to all this trouble for me!

"I wonder where my brother is?" Mandy said, breaking into my thoughts. "He's supposed to be helping with the food."

"Maybe he's down in the kitchen," I guessed. "Mark is one of the most reliable people around. I'm sure he's helping out." The Bennett family had lived next door to us for over fourteen years, so I knew Mark and Mandy very well. Since Mandy is my age and Mark and Peter are both two years older, the four of us had grown up together.

"I should be helping out in the kitchen myself," Mandy said, glancing at her watch. "I'm dying to know what you're going to wear, though, before I go."

I stepped over to the closet and thumbed

through the array of outfits. "I was planning to wear my denim skirt, but you have one on."

"Denim is too dull for the birthday girl," Mandy objected. "You should wear something bright so you're easy to pick out in the crowd—like your hot pink jumpsuit."

"The yard isn't that big. Anybody who wants to find me will have no trouble." I eyed Mandy with amusement. "And didn't you just tell me a minute ago that my lipstick was too bright?"

"The lipstick was all wrong," Mandy insisted. "But the jumpsuit would be a practical move. All the kids—with their gifts—will be able to spot you right away!"

"I'll give it some thought," I promised, laughing. Mandy never missed an angle. That was one of the things I loved about her.

I went downstairs about twenty minutes later, after I'd spotted my first guests, Becky Langer and John Wilson, down in the yard. They were the #1 happy couple at Fairmont High.

I felt a little uncomfortable about greeting my friends without Jeremy at my side—sort of like a half of a couple. But I had decided I was going to be my own person again, so I marched through the kitchen and out the back screen door with my head held high and a confident smile on my face.

At least I had had the good sense to ignore

Mandy's advice to wear something flashy. I'd chosen an outfit in which I felt at ease: my khaki walking shorts and a bright pink, over-size T-shirt. A happy medium between drab and neon.

"Happy birthday!" Becky and John chorused.

Little four-year-old Joy came rushing up in breathless excitement to take the present Becky was carrying, the plastic strands of Joy's grass skirt swishing around her stout little legs. "Mama said I could put these on the porch," she announced.

"That's fine," I said, giving her cheek a pinch. I shot a glance at Mandy, who was standing near the picnic table with a pitcher of lemon-ade. I pointed at Joy and winked. Mandy rolled her eyes in exasperation.

"Mama said you're s'posed to go in the garage and get a fortune 'fore anybody else," Joy reported.

"Oh, she did, did she?" I asked. Shielding my eyes against the sun, I peered at the garage located at the far end of the yard. The small service door was closed, and there was some kind of sign posted on it.

So far I'd had few details about the fortune-telling event. Mom knows how fascinated I am with romance and suspense and had come up with the idea as a special treat. She claimed that she was handling it all by herself—and she'd been acting secretive all week.

"I'd better check this out," I told Becky and John as I headed for the garage.

The sign on the door read *Karen Only*. I walked in and was surprised to find it quite dark inside. I blinked, trying to focus on my surroundings. What was Mom up to? I wondered. The windows were covered with newspaper, and the large door facing the alley was curtained with two old bedspreads. The only light in the room came from a single yellow bulb suspended on a wire from the rafters.

A woman was seated at a square table in the center of the concrete floor, just beyond the light. "Do come in," she said in a low voice.

I moved forward tentatively, uncertain of her identity. Naturally I'd expected my mother to be playing the gypsy, but this woman's voice was unfamiliar and her features were distorted in the shadows. Maybe a neighbor or a relative had been shipped in to throw me off the track, I thought.

But the woman staring at me was definitely unfamiliar, as was the cloudy crystal ball resting on an ornate ceramic pedestal in the center of the table.

"Sit down, please," the woman requested in a low, husky voice. I dropped into the folding chair opposite her.

"Who are you?" I asked uncertainly.

"I am Xaviera, the clairvoyant." There was a knowing glitter in her dark, deep-set eyes.

Xaviera looked like a genuine gypsy from a traveling carnival. A lime-green scarf was wound around her head. Her face was coated with dramatic makeup. She wore an orange blouse that buttoned at the throat, and a black lace shawl rested on her shoulders like a dark spider web. Gold hoops hung from her ears, and fine cords of black beads intertwined around her neck.

I groped for something to say. Nothing came to mind.

"You are here to celebrate your birthday, to learn the future," Xaviera said encouragingly. She lowered her gaze to the crystal ball on the table between us and began to move her hands over it in a circular motion. The cloudy ball took on an eerie glow as she murmured in low tones.

Was all of this really happening to me? I wondered. Was it a dream? My heart quickened as Xaviera's chanting picked up speed.

Suddenly she fell silent, dropping her hands to the cloth. She gazed into the crystal with narrowed intensity.

"What do you see?" I croaked.

She raised her eyes to meet mine. "I see a challenging summer ahead for you. Your life is changing drastically as you attempt to assert your independence. It won't be easy . . . people are not always what they seem. I see hidden feelings in those around you. Those struggling to influence you are determined."

I had always been fascinated by fortune-telling, but I wasn't certain that I believed in it. I had to admit, though, that this woman seemed to know her business. "You are right," I told her. "Do you see anything else?"

"I see wheels. Rolling wheels."

"I do want to get my driver's license," I said.

"Does pizza mean anything to you?" Xaviera inquired.

"I like mine with pepperoni and mushrooms," I replied. "But other than that . . ." I paused in thought. "My ex-boyfriend Jeremy and I spent a lot of time at Romano's Pizza Nook this past year."

"Perhaps," Xaviera said, her eyes intent on the crystal. "There is an overwhelming aura of love surrounding you," she continued. "A young man very near us—certainly on the premises— loves you very deeply."

"Wow!" I gasped in delight. Believing in clair-voyance was getting easier by the minute. "Who is it?"

Xaviera shrugged. "I do not see his face. I feel his presence. Perhaps you already know who it is." She watched me expectantly.

"Uh, no," I admitted sheepishly. "I—I'm unattached right now, so this mystery man has every opportunity to step forward now."

"He must have his reasons for subtlety. But keep your eyes and ears open," she said. "There will surely be signs."

"Because you see signs?"

"No." Xaviera smiled for the first time. "Because I know teenage boys."

I had the feeling that Xaviera's last statement was a dismissal of sorts, but I was determined to detain her. "As long as you have your crystal lit up and everything, I—"

"You are concerned about asserting your independence."

"Right! You really are good!"

"The best," she said simply. "Give me your palm. That will tell us much." I extended my hand. Xaviera held it palm side up under the glow of the crystal ball for a careful inspection. "Your hand is long and flexible, with tapering fingers."

"Is that good?"

"It means you have a sensitive, creative nature —more impulsive than methodical, I'm afraid." Xaviera studied my palm intently. "Your headline is long and straight, which means you are shrewd and a good planner. Your line of fate is curved toward the mount of Jupiter, which indicates success through effort."

"Sounds like I'm in pretty good shape," I said with relief.

But a slight frown crossed over Xaviera's face. "Your heartline is very strong—even stronger and longer than your headline. That means that the heart often rules the head."

"Is there anything you can tell me for certain?" I asked.

"You are a smart young lady with a big heart. Try to balance your emotions with good sense. I am certain you can do it." Xaviera released my hand abruptly. "The reading is over."

Most of my guests had arrived by the time I stepped dazedly back out to the sun-drenched lawn. Music throbbed from the stereo set up on the back porch, mingling with talking and laughter. Dad was standing at the barbecue in a billow of smoke, turning hamburgers and hot dogs with a long spatula. Peter was organizing a crowd eager to test their skill at his ring-toss booth. Tiffany was performing magic tricks for a semicircle of enthusiastic kids. Mandy was at the picnic table, arranging bowls of snacks with Joy at her heels. Everyone seemed to be carrying on as if this was a regular party.

Of course it *was* a regular party to all of them, I reminded myself. Only my pulse was racing from my encounter with Xaviera.

I scanned the crowd, wondering who my mystery match might be. I half-hoped someone would burst forward through the commotion, sweep me into his arms, and kiss me passionately, but no one seemed to be coming my way.

"Karen?"

I turned my head at the sound of a masculine voice—and my knees began to weaken. I was gazing into the gorgeous brown eyes of Fairmont High's star quarterback.

"Yes, Rich?" I managed to ask.

"Happy birthday," he said.

"Thanks," I said shyly. "Did you bring Abby with you today?"

"Uh, no," Rich replied. "We had a blowup last night. You know how it goes." He sounded pretty uncomfortable.

"Yeah, I just went through something like that with Jeremy." I wondered if Rich was my mystery man. If so, Xaviera certainly provided prompt delivery with her predictions.

"Karen, I was just wondering . . ." His voice trailed off.

"What, Rich?" I prompted softly.

"Your dad is really burning those burgers over there—that barbecue is like a towering inferno! Could you speak to him about cooking a medium rare one for me? Maybe if he nursed it along slow on the edge of the rack, away from the flames—"

"So you can't take the heat, Rich?" I murmured under my breath.

"Huh? I'm talking about the *burgers*, Karen," Rich said, looking puzzled.

"I'll speak to him right now, Rich," I promised, forcing a smile. After all, Rich wasn't responsible for my letdown. He didn't know I was expecting so much more.

I relayed Rich's request to my dad and then strolled through the crowd talking to my friends. As soon as I could break away, I headed for the refreshments to tell Mandy about Xaviera.

"I have to go talk to her!" Mandy exclaimed, swallowing the last of her hot dog in one gulp.

"Wait," I pleaded as she dashed across the yard. "I need your help in finding my mystery man."

"I need one of my own first," she called back laughingly before disappearing through the garage door.

Mandy reappeared about ten minutes later. I waved to her from Peter's booth, and she made a direct beeline for me. "Very funny, Karen," she complained. "Very funny."

"What's the matter? Did Xaviera tell you to join a monastery?"

"Genuine clairvoyant, eh?" Mandy took my arm. "Foggy crystal and palm reading, eh? Let's go have a chat with her together."

"I don't understand—"

"Your fascination for mystical adventures has finally driven you over the edge, Karen. The only palms that woman knows anything about sway in the Miami breeze."

I couldn't believe my eyes when I re-entered the dark garage. If the table with the bright red cloth on it hadn't still been in place, I would have sworn that I'd dreamed the whole fortune-telling episode!

Chapter Two

"Your destiny awaits you!"

The woman beckoning me into the garage this time bore an incredible resemblance to Charo. She was wearing a black peasant blouse pulled down to reveal a lot of bare shoulder, a flowing blond wig with a bandana tied over it, and about five pounds of jewelry.

"Mom!" I sank down once again in the folding chair, glancing briefly at Mandy, who was standing off to the side. Mandy was wearing her you're-quite-the-joker expression.

"Not Mom," Mom objected, lifting a heavily penciled brow. "My name is Gypsy Rosalee, psychic vonder of the vorld," she said in a heavy, phoney accent.

I glanced down at the crystal ball. But it wasn't a crystal ball anymore. I was now staring into an upside-down fishbowl.

"Mom—uh, Gypsy . . ." I began to protest, but then I decided not to spoil her act. Her face was screwed up in concentration, and she was rubbing the sides of the fishbowl so hard that it squeaked. It was obvious that she was thoroughly enjoying herself.

"A vonderful summer lies ahead for you," she said, searching the fishbowl intently. "A job is on the horizon." I could have guessed that was coming. Her thinking was more wishful than mystical.

"Any boys, Gypsy?" I asked.

"Some dating," she answered with a shrug.

"Later curfew?" I probed, struggling to keep a serious expression.

Gypsy Rosalee moaned in agony. "Nooo. Young girls need beauty sleep!"

"See anything else?"

"Help your mother with housework. Keep bedroom clean."

"Sounds a lot like my fortune," Mandy interrupted, leaning over to rap on the fishbowl. "Maybe this thing has a short circuit."

"I'm sure your mother will thank me," Mom said brightly in her normal voice. "Well, how was I?"

"Great," I assured her. "But what happened to Xaviera?"

"Who are you talking about, Karen?" Mom said. She sounded genuinely perplexed.

17

"She was sitting in here half an hour ago," I explained. "Right where you are now."

"I didn't see anyone. I came in from the alley." She gestured to the bedspreads shielding the double-door entrance. "I was delayed because I'd misplaced my fishbowl. I had to rush down to the pet store and buy another one. I was just setting up when Mandy walked in."

"This is sort of spooky!" Mandy said dramatically.

"Not really spooky," I said. "Strange, maybe—"

"Tell me exactly what happened," Mom interrupted.

I quickly told her my story, then asked, "Do you think someone took your first fishbowl to delay you?"

"Of course not!" Mom exclaimed. She thought for a second. "Well, I suppose it's possible."

"Let's check the alley," Mandy suggested.

We rushed outside, pushing aside the bedspreads. The only person in the alley was Mandy's brother Mark. His orange Charger was just rolling to a stop in front of the Bennett garage next door.

"Where've *you* been?" Mandy demanded breathlessly, jerking open the driver's door. "Delivering the fortune-teller back to her camp, I bet!"

Mark stared at her, then laughed. "Yeah, yeah, sure. I dropped the fortune-teller off and picked up the leprechaun. C'mon, I'll show you." He walked to the back of the car and opened the trunk. "Oh, leprechaun, come out now. We're here."

"This is serious, Mark," I told him earnestly. "We're looking for a woman who told my fortune a little while ago."

Mark ran a hand through his curly black hair. "That was your mother, Karen," he informed me patiently. He shook his head. "I can't believe her disguise was that good."

"Mark, where *have* you been?" Mandy asked. "You're supposed to be helping with Karen's party."

"I am helping." Mark reached into the trunk, pulled out a grocery bag, and thrust it into Mandy's arms. "Mr. Daly sent me to the supermarket. The food is disappearing at an alarming rate."

"Sorry, Mark," I apologized, feeling my cheeks heating up. "Guess we got carried away."

"This fortune-teller must have told you some pretty dynamite stuff, huh?" Mark looked really interested.

"Sort of," I answered evasively. "I'm not sure she was for real, though."

"A little magic never hurt anybody," Mark said with a conspiratorial wink. "Especially on your birthday."

"Maybe you're right." I really had nothing to lose by having a little faith in the old woman.

And believing that a boy nearby was madly in love with me was certainly a fate I could handle with no problem!

I went back to the party and headed for the picnic table. Having my fortune told twice had given me an appetite!

I leaned against one of the huge oak trees and bit into a hamburger. Someone had temporarily shut off the radio, and Joy was doing her baby hula routine in the gazebo to the tinny sound of a 45 rpm record.

"Hello, Karen."

The familiar voice startled me. I set my plate down on a nearby table before it tipped over in my shaky hands. Jeremy Miller had done it. He'd shown up uninvited.

"Hi, Jeremy." I didn't make a move toward him. Having the solid one hundred year old tree to lean back on made me feel more secure.

"Happy birthday," he said, flashing his most endearing smile. "Mad, Karen?"

"About my birthday? No, it's the nicest one I've ever had."

"You know that's not what I mean," Jeremy said, his tone impatient.

It was tough to look directly at Jeremy's handsome face and not melt a little. His dark blond hair was full of sun streaks, and he had a good start on a summer tan—both amazing feats, considering the hours he spent hanging around dimly lit Romano's Pizza Nook. I was surprised to see that he'd had the good sense to leave his favorite leather jacket at home. He was dressed for the California heat in a blue T-shirt and nice jeans.

"It was a hard decision—about whether to invite you, I mean . . ." I trailed off uncomfortably.

"I didn't come to make trouble," he assured me. "I bought your present before we broke up, so I thought I'd run it over." He handed me a brightly wrapped package and shrugged. "Seemed like the thing to do. I don't have any use for a bottle of your favorite perfume or a Cyndi Lauper cassette."

"Well, thanks," I said, casually looking around. I noticed a few people at the party watching us. I felt as if we were two department store mannequins in a storefront window. To make matters worse, there was no background music to drown out our conversation. Joy's hula act was over, and nobody had turned on the radio again.

"I really miss you," Jeremy blurted out suddenly.

"It's only been a couple of weeks," I pointed out in a low tone. I glanced around pointedly at my guests. "They're all just looking for a dramatic scene to talk about on the beach tomorrow, you know," I whispered.

"That's fine with me," he said, much to my surprise. "We *belong* together, Karen."

My good sense immediately cried out "no."

21

But what if he was right? I had to know if he had arrived in time to be counted in Xaviera's fortune. "When did you get here, Jeremy?"

"I—I don't know the exact minute," he replied.

"Five minutes? Ten minutes?" I prodded.

"Longer than that. I was hanging around out front for quite a while." Jeremy watched me with a puzzled expression. "What difference does it make?"

"Oh, it's nothing important," I hedged. But of course it was. If I chose to believe Xaviera's fortune, it could make all the difference in the world.

Jeremy was looking at me strangely. I guess he had no idea what I was talking about. How could he?

"So what do you say?" he asked. "Is it okay if I stick around here for a while?"

I sighed. "I really don't think so, Jeremy. I still need some time to think about us, and— and it might be easier for both of us if you leave." *Especially for me*, I added silently. "Thanks for coming by, though. It was really nice of you."

If Jeremy was mad, he didn't show it. "So I guess it's no use asking you to take back my ring."

"No, not right now. I'm sorry."

"You'll come around," Jeremy said. He squared his shoulders and walked away.

The party broke up at about four o'clock, shortly after I had opened all of my gifts. Everyone praised my family for putting on such a great extravaganza. Some of my friends couldn't resist needling me for not taking Jeremy's class ring back, though. I pretended to take it good-naturedly, but it hurt.

"Dinner is served," Mom said with exaggerated eloquence a couple of hours later.

Dinner that evening consisted of party leftovers at the picnic table. I passed out the cups and plates with "Sweet Sixteen" printed on them, and Tiffany brought silverware from the kitchen.

"Any potato salad left?" Peter asked, spooning some red Jell-O onto a plate. At one o'clock it had been a stiff, bell-shaped mold. Now it had the consistency of glue.

"I don't think so," Tiffany responded.

"Joan, you've forgotten the taco salad," Dad told Mom as he took a second inventory of the near-empty bowls and platters.

Mom glanced at the table. "There wasn't any left, honey."

Dad groaned in disappointment. "I've been looking forward to sampling it all afternoon. I was so busy at the barbecue, I didn't have a chance to eat much myself."

"There are only hot dogs here," Peter complained. "Weren't there any hamburgers left?"

"No," Dad replied, shaking his head in wonder. "I've never seen so much food consumed by so few. Twenty-five kids ate almost ten pounds of hamburger, three packages of hot dogs, taco salad, potato salad, Jell-O, and countless bags of chips and pretzels—then topped it all off with cake and ice cream!"

"There was a neighborhood conspiracy brewing here," Dad continued. "School's been out for a couple of weeks, and parents are already beginning to feel the strain on their grocery budgets. The day those birthday invitations arrived, Fairmont teenagers were coaxed into starving themselves in anticipation of loading up at the Daly bash."

Laughter erupted around the table.

"Look at it from a dentist's point of view, Dad," Tiffany suggested. "Maybe some of the stuff the kids ate will cause cavities and they'll end up in your office downtown having them filled."

"I would never wish that on any of our guests, but I must say a few of them could probably use braces," Dad remarked.

"Leave it to Dad to check out teeth at a party," Tiffany remarked with a chuckle.

"I know you had as good a time as anybody, Dad," I said as I ladled out some punch. "I saw you running in and out of the porch to put on Beach Boys tapes."

"Yeah," Peter chimed in. "He was teaching everybody dances from the sixties."

"I thought you were slaving over a hot barbecue all afternoon, Carl!" Mom exclaimed in surprise, staring at Dad over the rim of her paper cup. "While I was telling fortunes in that stuffy garage, you were doing the boogaloo around the gazebo."

"Speaking of dancing around the gazebo," Dad said, "where is our little hula baby?"

"She was poking around in the garage," Mom said. "I told her she could help me clean up. Joy!" Mom called over her shoulder. "Come for dinner!"

Joy came scampering out of the garage and across the lawn, still wearing her green hula skirt and red lei.

"Did you have a good time this afternoon?" I asked as she slid onto the bench beside me.

"Uh-huh. And I got a secret." Joy grinned, her blond curls bouncing as she bobbed her head.

"Hey, what's that on your ear, shrimp?" Peter asked, attempting to reach across the table at Joy.

"No!" she squealed. "It's mine! You can't have it!"

I cupped Joy's chin and turned her face toward me. A gold hoop was hanging from her earlobe. I recognized it immediately as belonging to Xaviera. Let them doubt me *now*, I thought smugly.

"Finders keepers!" Joy wailed as I gently pulled it from her ear.

"This belongs to Xaviera!" I announced, holding it up for all to see.

"Give it up, Karen," Peter muttered.

"I can't believe you couldn't see past Mom's disguise," Tiffany said, tossing her long blond mane behind her shoulders.

"You always did have a colorful imagination, Karen," Dad said proudly. "Of all our children, you're the one who's always taken things a step further."

"The woman was there in the garage," I insisted stubbornly.

"If you say so, Karen, I believe you," Mom soothed.

I gave my mother a smile. "Xaviera said that a boy at the party was madly in love with me. I wonder who it could be?" I was becoming obsessed with this. "Jeremy?"

"No!" the Dalys cried in unison, causing me to flinch. It's a rare occasion when the family agrees on an issue. I knew I had hit a brick wall. They never had liked Jeremy very much.

"C'mon, it was just a theory," I said defensively.

"If I did believe in this hocus-pocus, I'd tell you that she didn't mean Jeremy Miller," Tiffany declared. "I'm sure the fact that he's a jerk came through loud and clear in that crystal ball of hers."

"Jeremy has plenty of good points," I shot back.

"Since you dated him all during your sopho-more year, he must," Mom agreed. "But you know as well as we do, dear, that he wanted to monopolize your entire life."

"By spring he didn't even want you to come home for dinner!" Dad said.

"His mother works evenings, and he's on his own a lot," I said. I was accustomed to defend-ing Jeremy automatically.

Mom chimed in. "Jeremy has a good home, and he chooses to hang around Romano's Pizza Nook."

"He thinks he's James Dean or something," Tiffany said. "He wears that black leather jacket over to the Nook all the time. A rebel in two hundred dollars' worth of cowhide!"

"Rebel with a buck," Peter joked.

"Maybe Xaviera meant somebody else," I said at last.

"Maybe. If a fortune-teller went to the trouble of crashing your party and setting up her voo-doo stuff in our garage," Peter reasoned, jab-bing his fork in the air, "she wasn't aching to deliver a message about Jeremy Miller."

The rest of them agreed with Peter hands down. To my relief, Dad changed the subject.

Joy seemed to have forgotten the earring. I dropped the gold hoop into the pocket of my shorts, thinking that I'd like nothing better than to return it to its owner. If I found her, I'd coax her to gaze into her crystal until she could tell me the identity of the boy who loved me.

I had trouble falling asleep that night. Finally I got up at around midnight and began to jot down the names of all the boys who had attended the party. I felt better seeing their names in print. Somehow it made the search for my match seem more orderly. I'd start working on it first thing tomorrow.

I climbed back into bed more relaxed. I yawned widely, stretched out, and drifted right off into a dreamless sleep.

Chapter Three

Things began to wind back down to normal on Sunday. We all pitched in to get the yard cleaned up, and it was in pretty good condition by noon. Some problems would take more time to remedy, like the giant cola stain on one of the patio cushions. But I'm proud to say that Mom and Dad kept their cool through the whole morning—even when Becky Langer's mother called to report that Becky had misplaced her two-hundred-dollar watch. Mom turned white, but managed to assure Mrs. Langer calmly that we would make a thorough search.

We all combed the yard, but Peter was the one who came through. He discovered the watch near some shrubbery behind the gazebo.

"Victory!" he exclaimed, waving the watch above his head like a banner.

"Thank goodness, Peter," Mom cried with relief. "What a stroke of luck."

"Not really," Peter replied with a grin. "Becky Langer and John Wilson spent half the party back here in a clutch."

"Hush!" Mom warned, pointing at Joy.

"I remember them," Joy said, beaming. "They gave me a quarter just to go away!"

"Should've held out for more," Peter said, ruffling her blond curls with his hand.

"Peter!" Mom reprimanded.

"Just trying to teach her the value of a dollar," Peter said with a shrug. Peter thinks he's a financial expert just because he earns a healthy commission at Sid's Liquidators where he works with Mark.

"*We* will do that when the time comes," Dad said with finality.

The family scattered after lunch. Everyone had their own plans. I was no exception. Now that I was sixteen, I had new responsibilities. Finding a job was a top priority.

It's an unwritten rule in the Daly household that children sixteen and older do their best to find a summer job. I didn't want to be the first Daly who was an exception to that rule.

Peter, now eighteen, had spent the last two years working at Sid's Liquidators. Even though Mom and Dad get tired of listening to his super-salesman line, they're extremely proud of his good record there. Tiffany, at nineteen, is a head counselor at a day camp for pre-schoolers. She's won a couple of awards for innovative projects and all the kids love her.

I was up against a lot of sibling talent. Everyone was earning a salary but me. Even little Joy had managed to earn a quarter the day before. Sighing, I spread the want ad section of the Sunday paper out on the kitchen table. With a red marker in hand, I began to pore over the columns of available jobs.

"Hi in there!" I looked up to find Mandy peering in at me through the screen door.

"Come in," I said. "I need all the help I can get."

Mandy dropped into the chair beside me and winced at the sight of the ads. "I see turning sweet sixteen isn't so sweet after all."

"You're sixteen, too," I pointed out. "Aren't you going to look for a job?"

"I'm supposed to be," she admitted. "So far I haven't had much luck. Boy, if you beat me to it, my parents will hit the ceiling!"

I laughed. "Let's look at the ads together and fight over the best jobs."

"What have you circled here?" Mandy leaned over the paper.

"The dress shop in the Pine Crest shopping center is looking for a salesgirl. And—"

"Romano's Pizza Nook is looking for someone!" Mandy interrupted. "Karen, that's it!"

"Huh?"

"Your fortune, dummy. Xaviera said something about a pizza, remember?"

"Do you really think I should take her seriously?" I asked.

"Of course you should! I figured you'd be sitting here with a list of the boys who attended the party—not the crummy want ads, for Pete's sake."

"I'm curious, but I'm not *desperate*," I reprimanded her. "But I did make a list," I confessed. "I'll get it—and an earring Xaviera left behind."

I raced upstairs to my room and grabbed the list from my desk. Then I crossed over to my dresser and flipped open the lid of my jewelry box. To my amazement, the gold earring was gone. I flew back to the kitchen to tell Mandy.

"Gone?" Mandy's eyes grew wide. "This is really weird, Karen."

"Maybe I'm flipping out," I said in panic.

"You're as sane as I am."

"That's not much comfort!" I retorted.

Mandy rolled her eyes at me, but chose to ignore my comment. "Someone in your family must've taken it. Unless Xaviera has the power to summon objects. . . ." Mandy took in a sharp breath.

"This is really frustrating," I muttered. "I don't know what to think."

"Well, let's forget about the earring for now and assume that there's a boy out there waiting for your loving embrace. We'll take a look at the list together and narrow down the number of possible candidates." Mandy took my marker and crossed off Peter and Mark. "Who else can we cross off?" she pondered.

"John Wilson," I replied promptly. "He was so involved with Becky yesterday, he barely gave me a second glance."

"Are you sure? We don't want to go overboard with eliminations. Remember, this boy is hiding his feelings so his identity won't be obvious."

"No one can hide them that well," I protested with a laugh. I told her about Joy and the quarter.

"Okay," Mandy relented. "Bill Kennedy? He seems too engrossed in cars to fall madly in love with a girl, in my opinion."

"Better keep him on," I said. "Danny Sullivan dates girls between auto races."

Mandy nodded with a grin. "I saw Rich Feldon talking to you yesterday."

"He was only requesting a medium-rare burger," I said regretfully.

"I think we'd better keep him on the list for the time being," Mandy said after some consideration. "He and Abby are on the outs. Who knows? Maybe he isn't in touch with his feelings yet."

After another half hour of deliberation, we came up with a list of several hopefuls, including Jeremy Miller. I figured he and I were through, but Mandy insisted that he qualified just the same, merely by being in the right place at the right time.

"Now, you have to apply at Romano's Pizza Nook tomorrow," Mandy said as she rose to leave. "It's part of your destiny. I'm sure of it."

"All of this seemed so mystical until that earring disappeared!" I said.

"It's possible that Xaviera used her powers—"

"I don't know about that. My family probably hired her from a theater group in town," I snapped. "Of course they felt obligated to take the earring from my jewelry box and return it to Xaviera. If that's true, and she is an actress, that means my fortune is a hoax." I sighed. "That means there's no sense in my bothering to hunt for my mystery match, or rushing down to Romano's Pizza Nook to apply for a job. I'd be much better off answering the dress shop's ad. That job would probably be a lot less strain, and I wouldn't come home smelling like pepperoni every day."

"*Please* give this a try," Mandy implored. "If

the fortune turns out to be true, you can tell your grandchildren about it!"

"Okay," I said. "But I think I'm going to do a little investigating tonight into the missing earring business."

"Karen, are you crazy?" Tiffany glared up at me from the living room carpet. I admit I must have looked a bit strange, standing in the doorway with her Michael J. Fox poster.

"No, I've never felt better," I answered with a sweet smile.

"Oh, I get it. You want a poster like that for your birthday," she surmised.

"No thanks. Rob Lowe is more my type," I said.

"Too bad he wasn't at the party. Then you could add him to your list of possible matches. It would certainly add a little zing to that drab group."

"Were you nosing around in my stuff?" I demanded, thinking of the missing earring.

"The list was on your desk," Tiffany said defensively. "Can't blame me for happening to see it. I was returning a pencil I'd borrowed from you."

"Oh. Well, since we're on the subject, I'm sure you won't mind swearing on Michael here that you had nothing to do with hiring Xaviera."

"Swear on Michael J. Fox?" Tiffany repeated

in feigned shock. "Won't you just trust me if I say I'm innocent?"

"I'd prefer the Fox oath," I persisted. "If the earring hadn't disappeared, I wouldn't be so suspicious that a family member was involved."

"I didn't know the earring was gone," Tiffany assured me, jumping up to snatch the poster from my hands. "So get lost."

I stomped back up the stairs in search of Peter, my next target. Some of his good clothes were set out on his bed, and the bathroom door was shut.

"Peter?" I rapped on the door. "I have to talk to you."

His muffled voice called out "Shower," and then I heard the sound of the jet spray.

I headed back down the hall. As I passed his bedroom door, an idea struck me. I went inside, grabbed the shirt resting neatly on the bed, and darted for my room. I'd hold his shirt as hostage!

I sat on my bed, listening to his progress: the spray of the shower, the hum of the blow dryer, and the buzz of Dad's electric razor forging through any patches of peach fuzz. Finally he was out.

"Karen?" Peter's bare feet slapped against the hardwood hallway. "Have you seen my gray shirt?" Now he stood before me bare-chested in his gray pants, smelling of after-shave.

"I'm an expert on the subject of your shirts," I replied dryly, "I've ironed them often enough."

"You get paid," Peter reminded me. "Look, my shirt is missing. The gray one with the yellow pinstripes. I could've sworn I laid it out with my pants."

"It's available," I responded airily.

"Huh?"

"I want to trade it for some straight answers."

"Karen, what kind of game is this? I have to work tonight and I'm running late as it is. Mark will be here any minute. If we're not on time, Sid will have our hides. The store is having a Moonlight Madness sale and all the employees have to be on the floor by seven o'clock."

"It's simple, Peter. The earring is missing. I want to know if you took it."

"What earring?" Peter asked.

"Xaviera's."

"So we're back to worrying about that old gray-haired voodoo woman again!"

"Ah-ha! You just slipped up. I never said she had gray hair!"

"You must've, Karen. If there really was a fortune-teller—and I sincerely doubt there was—she could have done this family a big favor by steering you toward a summer camp for the lovelorn!"

"All right, I give up." I slid off my bed, lifted

my pink comforter, and pulled his shirt out from underneath.

"It's wrinkled!" Peter exclaimed. "Why didn't you stash it in your closet if you wanted to play games?"

"I was in such a hurry to hide it, I guess I didn't really think about it," I told him apologetically.

Peter sighed, putting an arm around me. "You've been hooked on romance and mystery ever since you were a little kid. What are we going to do with you, Kiddo," he teased.

"I just want to know if Xaviera was a *real* fortune teller," I said with a sniff.

"Exciting, isn't it?" Peter grinned devilishly.

I poked him in the stomach with my elbow. "Ouch!" he yelped. "My advice is that you stop asking so many questions and go with the flow. Who knows, it might be a lot of fun."

"Maybe you have a point," I said. "I'll just relax and let it happen."

"Now, about my shirt. I think—"

"You think you can wear something else," I supplied.

"I think you can run down to the kitchen and iron it while I put on my socks."

"Okay. And I'll be a good sport and only charge you my *regular* fee even though it's after my ironing hours."

"Since you sat on it, I think you should iron it for free," Peter argued.

"Half price," I bargained.

"Get going," Peter said, waving me on.

As I lugged the ironing board out of the broom closet, I made a solemn promise that I'd be a lot more careful about what I sat on in the future. Ironing the same shirt over again for half price was a dumb waste of time.

Just as the iron began to steam, Mark showed up at the screen door. "Oh, hi, Mark," I said. "Peter will be ready in a minute."

"Emergency job, I bet," he said, sliding down onto one of the oak chairs at the table. Mark looked nice. He was wearing navy-blue chinos and a red and gray plaid shirt. His curly black hair had a crisp, clean look and his gray eyes sparkled silver in the light.

"Peter's waiting for it," I responded simply. I didn't want to discuss the humiliating details. Mark was almost like a second brother, but there's always a fine line that separates friends from family members.

"Great party yesterday," he said, breaking into my thoughts.

"Wonderful," I agreed. "Thanks for helping out, Mark. I really appreciated it."

"Happy to do it."

"Too bad you don't know anything about that

fortune-teller," I ventured. "This mystery is driving me crazy!"

"Yeah, sorry about that." Mark's face registered regret, but his lips held the hint of a smirk. I felt as if he and Peter would be making fun of me later that night, and I didn't like it.

"She really was there," I asserted, glancing from him to the oxford collar on the board. "Ouch!"

"What happened?" Mark jumped up.

"I jabbed the tip of the iron into my hand. I hate these button-down collars!"

Mark took my burned hand and led me over to the sink. "Best thing to do is soak it in cold water," he said, turning on the faucet.

"Hey, what's going on, Mark?" Peter asked with an amused expression, leaning against the doorjamb. "Some kind of belated birthday ritual? Or have you taken up palm reading too?"

To my surprise, Mark actually began to blush under his tan. "She burned herself ironing *your* shirt," he shot back, dropping my hand like a sizzling coal.

"Ah-ha! The old 'I'm-burning-cool-me-off trick," Peter teased. "My shirt ready?"

"Yes," I said coolly, dabbing my hand with a towel.

Peter grabbed the shirt from the board and slipped it on. "Your hand okay?"

"It's fine," I said.

"Karen really is on the spot when you need a shirt, isn't she?" Mark observed.

"Yeah, she's on top of things all right," Peter agreed, flashing me an infuriating grin. I was afraid that he was going to tell Mark I'd sat on his shirt, but luckily he didn't.

"These Moonlight Madness sales at Sid's must keep you pretty busy," I said, eager to change the subject.

"Pretty busy," Peter replied.

"Depends on the merchandise Sid is trying to push," Mark added. "Stereo equipment and bicycles always go fast."

"Say, maybe I should apply for a part-time job at Sid's if the Romano job falls through tomorrow," I said with sudden inspiration.

"No!" Peter's answer was quick and definite.

I glanced at Mark. To my surprise, he looked just as negative.

"Togetherness can be pushed too far," Peter said adamantly. "Right, Mark?"

"If you go down there, Mandy will too." Mark shuddered slightly. "I couldn't stand that. She'd be bossing me around, reporting all my moves to Mom. Sorry, Karen. No way."

"Well, if you guys feel that strongly about it . . ."

My surrender brought huge smiles.

They took off in a hurry. Peter was still fumbling with his tie.

I couldn't believe it. After all my trouble, neither Tiffany nor Peter had given me any clues in my fortune-teller mystery.

When Mr. Romano opened the front door to the Pizza Nook Monday afternoon, I was on hand—along with several other job hopefuls. It was easy to distinguish them from the customers. Like me, they were wearing their good clothes.

People who hung out at the Nook were usually dressed pretty casually. It's just that kind of place. The walls are covered with old wood paneling, and the floor is checkered with square black and white tiles. There's an old jukebox positioned near the front door, and a video game beside it. The tables and chairs in the center of the room are made of cracked vinyl and scarred wood, and there are a few dimly lit booths running along both of the side walls. A large order counter spans the back, and beyond it a bright, narrow kitchen is visible through a rectangular opening in the wall.

The Nook is only two blocks away from Fairmont High, so it's a convenient place for students to hang out after school. Most of the restaurant's success is due to Mr. Romano. He takes all of our noise and laughter in stride and charges only a two-dollar minimum per customer. In return, he expects cooperation. No fighting or alcohol is allowed. And, he also makes a super pizza.

"All those interested in applying for the job should fill out an application," Maria Romano, the owner's plump black-haired daughter, announced. She set a stack of forms and some pens on the counter near the cash register. "My father will speak to each of you individually." After a few moments, she motioned to Mr. Romano, who was seated in the last booth in the corner puffing on a cigar and sipping coffee.

I leaned against the counter, absently biting on the tip of my pen. Did babysitting count as a previous job? I decided it did. Keeping an eye on a live wire like Joy should count for something. I filled in the small space provided for past experience.

"Well, hi, Karen!"

I whirled around to find Rich Feldon standing behind me in a pair of tan pants and a royal blue pullover. Definitely job-hunting clothes. "So you're interested in the job, too, huh?"

"How did you know?" he asked.

"Lucky guess," I said with a laugh. Rich is a great-looking guy and a wonderful quarterback, but he's definitely the blue-jeans-and-track-shoe type—for all occasions.

"Great party on Saturday. I had a wonderful time."

43

"Did you ever get your medium rare hamburger?" I asked.

"Oh, yeah, thanks." He smiled at me, his brown eyes warm. "Say, I was wondering. Since you aren't seeing Jeremy anymore and I'm through with Abby . . . I wondered if we could go out sometime."

Maybe he was my mystery match after all! "Hey, I'd like that," I replied, trying to sound casual even though my heart was soaring. There *was* life after Jeremy! "When?"

"How about tonight?" Rich suggested. "We could take in a movie. There's a new one at the Uptown."

"I'll have to check with my folks, but I'm pretty sure it'll be all right."

"Next, please," Mr. Romano called out briskly in his heavy Italian accent.

"Go ahead," Rich invited.

"No, I'll call home while you go for the interview."

I asked Maria if I could use the phone on the counter and dialed quickly. "Hello, Mom?"

"Did you get the job, dear?"

"Not yet, Mom. Can I go out with Rich Feldon tonight?"

"He didn't give you much notice, did he?"

"It's just a movie. Besides," I whispered, cupping my hand over the mouthpiece, "he may be the *one*, and I don't want to pass up the chance."

"The one what, dear?"

44

"My mystery match!" I said, a bit more sharply than I'd intended. "You know, the fortune-teller."

"Karen . . ." There was a pause, then my mother sighed. "I hope you're not taking this fortune business too seriously."

"This isn't a heavy commitment or anything, Mom. It's just a movie. Maybe we'll get a malt or something afterwards."

"Well . . . at least—"

"At least it isn't Jeremy this time," I supplied.

Mom laughed. "Okay. Go ahead and accept. But Karen, take my advice—next time play it cool and ask for at least forty-eight hours' notice."

"Twenty-four hours would be cool enough!" I protested. "But thanks, Mom."

"Goodbye, dear."

"It's all set," I told Rich when he joined me a few moments later.

"Good," was all Rich said.

He looked a little peaked. "How did it go?" I asked, nervous about my own interview.

"He's a tough guy," Rich shook his head forlornly. "If I knew anything about ladies' clothing, I'd go apply at the dress shop in the Pine Crest shopping center."

"Oh, Rich, you're exaggerating."

He smiled as if pitying my ignorance. "I'll pick you up around seven," he said, shuffling toward the entrance with his hands in his pockets. "And good luck!"

"Good afternoon, Karen," Mr. Romano said as I slid into the booth across from him a few minutes later.

"Good afternoon, sir," I said, handing him my application.

He spent some time examining my qualifications and puffing thoughtfully on his cigar. "I heard about your party," he said unexpectedly.

"You did?" I gulped, wondering if he was annoyed that we didn't order pizzas from him. But he wasn't. "Did you really have a fortune-teller?" he asked.

I nodded my head.

"Great idea. I could use someone like your gypsy to generate publicity. Perhaps I could hire her to come here one Saturday. . . ."

Of course I had to tell him I didn't know who—or where—she was.

"I'll put a sign on my bulletin board in front. Maybe someone will let her know," he said, dismissing the subject. "Now, about your qualifications."

My moment of truth was here. "My, uh, qualifications—" I began to stammer.

"Don't be so nervous," Mr. Romano chided. "True, you don't have any experience in the pizza business. But what most of the kids who came here today don't realize is that I'm not looking for somebody who makes pizza twice a week, or has a crust recipe that's been handed down through ten generations. I can train the person I hire. I *am* looking for a levelheaded kid who can follow instructions and can be depended upon. I have an advantage over many employers, you know. I've had the chance to watch my potential staff when they have nothing at stake. Of all the applicants today, you are the most well behaved on a day-to-day basis."

"I'm a very hard worker," I told him.

"I believe that, Karen," he said. "That is why I am offering you the job."

"Thank you so much!" I exclaimed. I was going to follow the Daly tradition after all!

"This position involves many duties," he continued. "Making pizzas, selling pizzas, cleaning up—and of course, delivering pizza. You will drive my delivery car. Of course, you can assure your parents that you will only deliver to the regulars I know well. And only during the lunch rush when you're really needed." He paused, read my expression, and asked the fatal question. "You *do* drive, don't you?"

"Not exactly," I murmured. "I mean, not yet. I've completed the classroom training. Now that I'm sixteen, I'll be going ahead with the behind-the-wheel phase."

Mr. Romano looked deflated. "We can work around it for a while, I suppose—that is, if you go ahead and start making arrangements for the lessons right away."

I agreed, but I didn't feel very happy about it. I already knew for certain that no one in the family wanted to teach me how to drive. And I wasn't sure I'd feel comfortable with them anyway. Xaviera had mentioned something about wheels in my fortune. Too bad she hadn't located a licensed driver with unlimited patience in that crystal ball of hers.

Chapter Four

I heard Rich's Chevy rattle to a stop in front of the house that night as I was finishing my makeup. Quickly I brushed my cheeks with one last stroke of blush and went to the top of the stairs to see who was going to answer the door. I leaned over the banister just in time to see Mom invite Rich inside.

I watched petite Mom—chattering enthusiastically—pull the tall, broad-shouldered quarterback into the entryway below. Rich looked very uneasy towering over her as she talked on about the weather and how much I was looking forward to the date. He avoided her gaze completely, shoving his hands into the pockets of his faded jeans and nervously kicking the tip of his Nike into the tiled floor.

How could Mom do this to me? I wondered, shaking my head with a mixture of embarrassment and irritation. What if Rich thought I was so desperate for a date that my mom had to latch on to the first boy who rang our doorbell?

Of course, I knew she was doing it because she was anxious to welcome any replacement for Jeremy Miller. But to my surprise, her actions caused defiance to flash inside me. If Jeremy was my destiny, she'd have to accept it. Everyone would have to accept it!

Common sense took over as I grabbed my purse then started down the stairs. I wouldn't run back to Jeremy because I was mad at my mother for poking into my love life. I wasn't going to settle for less than I deserved.

Relief crossed Rich's face the moment he spotted me. "Hi, Karen, you look great," he said, scanning me from head to toe.

"Thanks, Rich." I'd only chosen pale blue cotton jeans and a pink knit shirt, instead of a dressier outfit—but I'd done it for a reason. I'd seen Rich at the movies with Abby dozens of times during the school year. His clothes were always the same: football jersey, track shoes, and faded jeans. Abby was in the habit of dressing up for their dates, and I had always thought the two of them looked kind of silly together. I wanted everything to be perfect for our first date.

Rich sighed deeply as we climbed into his ancient Chevy a few minutes later. "Whew! Jeremy Miller must've really messed things up with your mother," he observed, with more insight than I'd have expected from him.

"Well, you know parents," I said, feeling a blush creeping up my face. "You're lucky Dad's answering service called him to the office with some kind of dental emergency. He wanted to welcome you, too."

Rich laughed. "Don't forget that I know all about having a steady," he said, pulling the car away from the curb. "Now take Abby, for instance. Mom loved her, but Dad thought she was bossy. Not that Dad hated her or anything like that," he added, a small smile playing at the corner of his mouth. "Nobody could hate a foxy girl like Abby."

I looked out the passenger window to hide a frown. As far as I was concerned, Rich's dad was right. Abby *was* bossy. But when a girl's beautiful, I guess she can get away with acting spoiled.

"This Chevy still runs pretty well," I said, hoping to change the subject.

"It gets me around," Rich said. "Abby always thought it was kind of cool."

My only reply was a feeble smile. Getting back into circulation was going to be a lot tougher than I had figured. Not only did I have to forget Jeremy's habits and adjust to different boys, but I had to adjust to their old girlfriends as well.

"This breaking up stuff is sort of rough," Rich said suddenly, as if he'd read my thoughts.

"It sure is," I agreed. "I think getting out of the house is a good idea, though. Nothing is more fun than watching a great movie with a huge bucket of popcorn."

"Yeah," Rich agreed, his brown eyes lighting up. "Popcorn with loads of butter." He soon pulled into the movie theater's crowded parking lot and parked in a space near the back. "I don't really need the butter, though," he continued. "Not everyone likes it. Abby hated having buttery fingers. She said no matter how many napkins I got, she still couldn't wipe the stuff off!" Rich chuckled fondly. "She's nuts."

As we walked across the parking lot, I discovered that Abby loved Cherry Coke, hated reruns, and used a clear brown soap on her face twice a day to keep it soft. This was far more than I ever wanted to know about the girl who'd stuffed Play Doh in my boots six times during a long winter in Miss Gardiner's second-grade class!

By the time we reached the theater lobby, I was forced to face it. Rich Feldon was not quite over Abby Pearson.

And Abby Pearson was not quite over Rich Feldon. She was already in the lobby, standing in the concession line with some of her friends. She was dressed in a silky red blouse and grey pants. She spotted us immediately—and sent me a lethal glare.

"Hey, Karen, you almost passed up the line," Rich exclaimed. He took my arm and guided me toward the concession stand.

It hadn't been an accident. I'd intended to slip into the dark theater before Rich saw Abby. Now we were trapped. She was only a few feet ahead of us.

"What can I get you, Karen?" Rich looked down at me, his brown eyes attentive and warm.

A bulletproof vest, I replied silently.

"Karen?"

"Nothing for me. I'm not really hungry."

"But you said you loved popcorn. Just like Abby—" Rich trailed off in embarrassment. He had suddenly realized that Abby was just up ahead, staring directly at him.

Abby had obviously heard what he'd said. She tossed her head in triumph, and her long dark hair rippled down her back.

"Let's skip the food," I suggested, pushing him out of line—no easy task, considering that he outweighed me by at least sixty pounds.

I heard later that the movie was pretty good, but personally I don't remember much of the plot. The evening hadn't begun too well, and seeing Abby had definitely ruined it. I couldn't wait to escape, and I nudged Rich out of his seat the minute the credits began rolling down the screen.

"Let's pick up a snack," Rich said as we crossed the parking lot in the cool summer night.

"We can walk over to Ice Cream Land," I said, pointing to the building across the street.

"That's a kiddie place," Rich objected. "Everybody else will be going over to the Pizza Nook."

"I know," I said grimly. "I'd like to avoid Abby if we can."

"You almost sound as if you've got something against her!" Rich said incredulously.

"Don't get so shook up," I soothed him, feeling as though I was slipping further and further into a bad dream. "Let's go across the street and talk about it."

The ice cream parlor was crowded with families. A middle-aged hostess met us at the entrance and led us to a pink-and-blue booth.

Rich planted his large forearms on the table between us and leaned forward. "Now, what's your problem with Abby?"

"Well, you haven't stopped talking about her all night long. And Abby looked ready to terminate me at the concession stand."

"She did?" Rich asked. Suddenly he looked like a hopeful 180-pound puppy with strands of brown hair falling in his eyes. A waitress stopped by our booth, and we paused to order two hot fudge sundaes.

"What is going on here, Rich?" I demanded over the background of squealing children. "If you're still hung up on Abby, you shouldn't have asked me out."

"But I thought you understood, Karen," Rich protested.

"Understood what?"

"About being alone. About being, you know . . . dumped." He hung his head sadly. I couldn't believe that the superjock of the school was reduced to such a lovesick mess.

"I was not dumped," I stated emphatically. "*I* broke up with Jeremy!"

"Oh. I guess I figured that a popular guy like him had—Oops, I'm sorry. That came out all wrong."

"Never mind," I said on a long sigh. "Here are our sundaes." *I should've known that Rich wasn't my mystery match in the first place*, I thought to myself.

It was shortly before ten o'clock when Rich pulled his Chevy back up to the curb in front of our house.

"Thanks for an interesting evening, Rich."

"I'm sorry about the mixup tonight, Karen," he said, resting his arm across my shoulders.

"I am too," I responded contritely. "I hope you understand. I'm not looking for someone to mope around with until my old steady comes back. I'm trying to branch out a little—meet new people."

"Guess I'm not into that scene at all," Rich admitted apologetically. "I miss Abby more every day. I just thought maybe we could wait around together. . . ." He trailed off sadly.

"Patch things up with her," I said.

"She's impossible!" he growled.

"So are you!" I laughed. "Why don't you go over to her house right now? It's still early."

"I'll think about it," Rich said.

"Great." I put my hand on the door handle and grabbed my purse.

"Karen, I hope we can go back to being friends," Rich ventured hopefully, "like we were before tonight."

"Well—"

"Hey, I promise to never ever ask you on another date as long as I live."

"In that case, we have a deal!" I agreed, laughing.

Rich walked me to my door. Naturally, the romantic kiss I'd envisioned sharing with my mystery man didn't happen. Rich rapped me lightly on the arm—the way he might greet a fellow football player—and jogged back to his car.

I slipped inside the house, feeling a little let down.

"Karen, you're home already?" Tiffany called

to me from the living room. "Come in here and tell us about your date."

I crossed the entryway and found Tiffany and Peter seated together on the living room sofa, a deck of cards spread out before them on the coffee table.

"Did Rich turn out to be your predicted match?" Peter quipped as I dropped onto the loveseat near the window.

"No, and I don't want to talk about it," I replied wearily, crossing my arms across my chest. "Who's winning the card game?"

"Tif, of course," Peter answered matter-of-factly, tossing his cards onto the table. "We've played seven hands, and she's aced me every time."

"I'm on a hot streak all right," Tiffany told me with satisfaction.

"It seems as though you can't lose at rummy ever since you added card tricks to that magic act of yours," Peter said.

"Sore loser," Tiffany said with a grin. She tossed her long blond hair over her shoulder and began to shuffle the deck with practiced ease.

"We always keep score when we play rummy," I pointed out. "Why don't you guys have some paper?"

Tiffany flashed Peter an odd look.

"I'm losing too badly to write it down," Peter said with a shrug.

"What happened between you and Rich, Karen?" Peter said. "I thought you'd be spilling everything the second you walked in."

"There isn't much to report," I said with a sigh.

"How about the punch?" Tiffany said suddenly.

"Now what do you mean?" I asked. The whole scene was really weird. What was everybody hiding?

"I made some of my special fruit punch, and we wondered if you wanted any," Peter explained, "Isn't that right, Tif?"

Suddenly I understood what was going on. "You aren't playing rummy at all!" I exclaimed, shaking a finger at the cards fanned in Tiffany's hands. "Tiffany, you dealt yourself more cards than you gave Peter. You were spying on me! You looked out the window and saw Rich punch my arm." I jumped up in fury. "I'll bet both of you were peeking through the window at us! You probably grabbed the deck of cards to cover your tracks when Rich left so quickly."

No one bothered to deny it.

"We were just looking out for our sister," Peter said after a moment.

"Right," Tiffany agreed. "We don't want to see you make another mistake the way you did with Jeremy. Just because Rich punched your arm instead of kissing you doesn't mean you should cross him off your list."

"Rich Feldon is not my mystery match," I declared firmly. I was still boiling over the fact that they had seen the silly exchange between the two of us.

"Maybe a little rap on the arm is his idea of sportsman's love," Peter suggested.

"A *big* rap on the arm could be my idea of sisterly love, brother." I shook my fist at him.

"I surrender!" Peter cried in mock-alarm.

"So do I!" Tiffany added. "No more meddling. Ignore our gold mine of experience. Mess things up on your own."

"Experience, eh?" I smiled smugly. "Neither one of you has been dating much lately, come to think of it. I'd say there isn't much gold in the mine."

"What is all the commotion about?" Dad asked standing in the doorway that led in from the dining room.

Mom was right behind him. "We could hear you bickering all the way from the kitchen."

"It's all settled," I assured them.

"I hope so," Dad said in his best no-nonsense tone. He and Mom sat down together on the sofa. "Now, if you children don't mind, your mother and I would like to watch the news in peace."

I stifled a yawn. "I'll need a good night's sleep

if I'm going to be fresh for my new job tomorrow," I said.

"I have a new tape I want to listen to in my room," Peter announced.

"Hey, wait a minute, everybody," I said, waving my hands to get their attention. "I just remembered that I'm going to need my driver's license if I'm going to hang on to my new job. Mr. Romano expects me to deliver pizzas at lunchtime. Anybody interested in helping me out?"

I scanned their faces for a glimmer of mercy, but I found only fear and panic. "Come on," I pleaded. "I'm not asking you to donate your bodies to science—"

"Might as well be," Peter cut in.

"When does Mr. Romano expect you to begin making deliveries?" Dad asked.

"As soon as possible," I replied. "One of you has to be willing to teach me the basics."

"Count me out," Tiffany declared. "I did my duty by teaching Peter. He cured me for life!"

"Getting in the car with a sister is a fate worse than death," Peter shot back with a hearty chuckle.

"Mom? Dad?" I appealed to them in desperation.

"Tiffany didn't speak to me for an entire week after I took her out on the road," Mom recalled with a frown. "I won't risk enduring another conflict like that."

"Me either. My ulcer has really been acting up lately," Dad said.

"What am I going to do?" I wailed. These were the same people who were dying to help me out with my dating situation. But when I asked them to volunteer for something I really needed. . . .

"We'll find someone else to do the job," Dad said. "There's no sense in putting that kind of stress on the family."

"Yeah," Peter agreed as I trudged up the stairs to my bedroom. "It's much smarter to torture an outsider."

Chapter Five

I went next door to Mandy's house first thing on Tuesday morning to fill her in on the gruesome details of my date with Rich. Mandy immediately sat me down in the wicker chair in the corner of her room.

"Is he the one, Karen?" she asked excitedly, pacing in front of me with her hands planted on her hips. I couldn't help but notice that she was a lot more dressed up than usual. Instead of her regular cutoffs and T-shirt, she was wearing a Laura Ashley skirt and white linen blouse. I suddenly felt sort of sloppy in my washed-out surfer shorts and short-sleeved sweatshirt.

"Karen," Mandy repeated impatiently, "tell me what happened!"

"All right, you asked for it." I told her everything—Rich's devotion to Abby, our snack at Ice Cream Land, and his good-bye gesture.

"What an awful night," Mandy murmured in sympathy. "Obviously he isn't your mystery match."

"I don't know where to go from here, Mandy," I admitted glumly. "Maybe I should drop the whole fortune thing."

"Don't give up now!" Mandy said, protesting, shaking her dark curly head. "Can't you see how well things are going—"

"How can you say that?" I interrupted with a groan. "Last night was pretty humiliating. I'll bet Abby Pearson really got a kick out of watching her old boyfriend and me bumble around the movie theater like a couple of idiots."

"You're ignoring some very important facts, Karen," Mandy insisted. "Parts of your fortune are already coming true. The pizza part, for instance. You landed the job at Romano's with no sweat. And the wheel part—from what you told me yesterday on the phone, it looks as though you're going to be making pizza deliveries behind the wheel of a car."

"If I get my license, that is," I put in. "No one in the family wants to give me lessons. And you know the summer-school driver's ed course was filled months ago."

"I have the same problem here," Mandy muttered. "But I just don't think you can brush off Xaviera's predictions just because of a few small setbacks."

"I'm not sure what to do next. How do you search for a boy who's supposed to be in love with you? Advertise on a billboard?"

"Working at Romano's Pizza Nook is even better than a billboard," Mandy pointed out excitedly. "All the boys from school hang out there, at least once in a while. You're bound to make contact with the right one sooner or later."

"Maybe," I said, brightening a little. "I'll give it a chance."

"Now you're talking," Mandy said, sitting down on the edge of the bed. She certainly wasn't her normal casual self. Instead of plopping down in the center of her bed—which was usually unmade—she carefully smoothed the already neat green-and-white gingham spread and sat gingerly on the edge of the mattress.

"Hey, why so dressed up?" I asked. By now I was bursting with curiosity.

"Well," Mandy began slowly. "I got the job at Flora's Dress Shop. Remember that ad in the Sunday paper?"

"Sure I remember. It was the ad *I* circled in red—the job you steered *me* away from."

"I was only thinking of your fortune, Karen," Mandy assured me. "If Xaviera had mentioned dresses, I would've pointed you in Flora's direction."

"I believe you," I laughed.

"Good," Mandy said with relief. "I'd hate to lose a best friend over a job."

"But why are you suddenly elegance plus?" I asked. "I know Flora has a dress code for her salesgirls, but she can't force you to make your bed!"

"I have to be neat for work from now on, so I decided it wouldn't hurt to clean up my act at home too," Mandy explained.

"I'll have to rent a formal just to come over here from now on," I teased, standing up to leave.

"I'm not totally reformed," Mandy corrected me, opening the drawer of her nightstand. "See, I have half a bag of cookies in here. The kind with the chewy centers."

"Whew," I said, pulling a chocolate chip cookie out of the plastic tray. "Thank goodness you're not completely over the edge yet."

"Mark is waiting downstairs to drive me to work. Want to ride along?"

I glanced at my watch. "I'd like to, but I don't have time. It's after ten already, and I have to go home and get ready for work myself."

"Now that we're career women, I guess we'll have to make some sacrifices," Mandy said as we walked down the stairs together.

Mark was standing at the front closet putting on his jacket. He smiled when he saw us coming. "Anything new on the fortune front?" he asked with a maddening smile.

I shrugged, hoping to evade the question. "Not—"

"For your information," Mandy interrupted smugly, "Karen already had a date with mystery-match candidate number one, Rich Feldon."

Mark shook his head in surprise. "That was quick work."

"I didn't work on him," I objected self-consciously. I couldn't believe that Mandy had even brought up such a humiliating subject to her brother.

"I didn't mean it that way," Mark hastily told me. "If you like him . . ."

"So what if her date was a horrible flop," Mandy rushed on staunchly in my defense before I could stop her. "It isn't her fault that Rich didn't even treat her like a date—just some sort of lovesick pal."

I tried to catch her eye, but it was no use. Sometimes, trying to stop Mandy from talking is like trying to stop a rushing river with a Dixie cup. Within seconds, Mark knew it all—right down to the chocolate topping on my sundae.

"I'm going home," I mumbled, heading out the front door.

Their voices drifted out through the front screens as I crossed the lawn.

"You embarrassed her with all that stuff, Mandy."

"*You* said she had to work on Rich to get a date!"

"But you told me all the private details."

"*You* wanted to know, Mark. You're pretty nosy, you know."

"Your mouth could easily hold the World Trade Center."

I have no idea how long they bickered about who'd humiliated me the most. As far as I was concerned, it was a tie.

I showed up at Romano's Pizza Nook thirty minutes later, ready to work out my troubles by kneading through mountains of pizza dough. I pictured myself in the spotless stainless-steel kitchen, pulling and pushing at mounds of the flour and water mixture. I'd be alone to dream and scheme about the summer ahead. Mr. Romano always started out new employees at the bottom of the pizza business—at the bottom of the pizza!

"Thank goodness you're early!" Mr. Romano boomed as I walked through the pizzeria's entrance. He was standing near the back counter beyond the tables and booths in his spotless white butcher's apron, his arms open wide in greeting.

"Me?" I asked blankly, looking around to see if he could be talking to anyone else. I hadn't expected to be considered so valuable on my first day.

"Yes, yes, Karen," he answered briskly. "My wife is having trouble with her back and won't be in today. Probably won't be in for a while, for that matter," he added half to himself. "Anyway, I'm going to have to give you my special crash course in how to serve up pizza Romano style."

That's why, instead of being holed up in the kitchen, I was forced out onto the floor with the boss's daughter Maria, carrying an order pad and wearing a brand new red Pizza Nook T-shirt instead of an apron.

"You look like a frightened rabbit," Mr. Romano said with a chuckle. It was just moments before opening time, and kids were already gathering on the sidewalk outside.

"I don't mean to," I said feebly, leaning against a booth. "It's just that this is more responsibility than I expected on the first day. I hope I can do a good job."

"I know it'll be a bit tough at first, but I warned you at the interview that you'd be up to your ears in every phase of the business. Unfortunately, you're being forced to handle some duties a bit quicker than usual, but you surely know my menu better than anyone. Right?"

"Right," I agreed, relaxing a little. "I'm familiar with every pizza you make, from the Sicily Sausage to Mama's Magic Mushroom."

"You see, Karen—I have a knack for spotting

levelheaded business types who can get the job done."

I figured this was no time to tell him that according to Xaviera's palm reading, my heartline was stronger than my headline. I just nodded my head and smiled.

Before long, the Nook was filled with the Fairmont High crowd, laughing, talking, and inhaling pizza and soda as fast as Maria and I could serve it. It's amazing how different everything looks from the waitress's point of view. Never before had I noticed how indecisive my friends could be when they were ordering food. They bickered about whether to get soda by the glass or pitcher, and how many different pizza toppings they wanted. As a customer, it had never seemed inconvenient to order a pizza with half sausage, half pepperoni, and anchovies on half the sausage and half the pepperoni. As a waitress, the crazy combinations made my head spin. Then there was the continuous thump of the jukebox in the background. I could just barely keep my orders straight. Maria assured me that all of it would soon become second nature—that in no time I'd be able to separate the orders from all the noise. I just hoped my headline was long enough to handle it!

The crowd thinned out by mid-afternoon. I found myself looking forward to my two-thirty break with pathetic longing. The idea of slipping off my shoes for fifteen minutes meant more to me at that moment than all the riches of the world.

"Do you mind if I take my break first?" Maria asked as we cleaned one of the front booths near the pane glass window facing the street.

"No, I can hang on for a while," I told her.

"I have an important phone call to make," Maria explained, a smile on her round, pleasant face. "You can have your break first tomorrow." She picked up the gray plastic tub of dishes on the table behind us and wove her way across the black-and-white floor to the kitchen in back.

I continued to wipe down the cracked vinyl seats, concentrating on doing a good job. When I glanced out the window all of a sudden, I had the misfortune to catch sight of Abby Pearson out on the sidewalk with a couple of her best friends. She positively glared at me through the glass. In her orange jumpsuit, with her long black hair fanned across her shoulders, she reminded me of a tigress.

Naturally, I hoped that she and her friends would pass by without stopping in—and naturally, they made a beeline for the door, with Abby in the lead. They took a table in the center of the room, laughing and whispering among themselves.

"Waitress! *Oh, waitress!*" Abby said in a singsong voice. She raised an arm heavy with golden bracelets.

I reluctantly approached their table, fervently hoping that Rich had patched things up with her last night. "Can I get you something?" I asked politely.

"This table is sticky," Abby complained, her full lips set in a pout.

I knew very well that she hadn't even touched the tabletop yet, but I played along and wiped the surface for the second time in the past ten minutes.

"What a shame that a Daly had to settle for a grubby job like this," Abby remarked snidely as I worked. "Tiffany has that great thing going at the kiddie camp, and Peter is an ace salesman at Sid's. Too bad."

"This is a good job," I said with dignity. "Good enough for Rich," I couldn't help adding. "He applied for it too."

"Why don't you guys go put on some lip gloss," Abby said to her friends with a significant expression. Like obedient children, they immediately headed for the ladies' room.

"Who do you think you are, Karen Daly, stealing my boyfriend?" Abby hissed, looking around to make sure no one important from school was watching her losing her cool. Abby had built her whole reputation on being very, very cool.

She wasn't about to spoil it blowing up at a nobody like me.

"Rich asked *me* out," I said in a low voice. I was eager to hold my temper too because I wanted to keep my job. Mr. Romano wouldn't be very happy about catching me fighting with a customer on my first day.

"Everybody knows we didn't really break up!" Abby snapped.

"Everybody in *your* crowd, maybe," I shot back defensively. "You really have nothing to worry about, Abby. Rich wants you back. He told me so last night. Besides, he's not my type at all."

A flicker of relief crossed her face. "Not that I was really worried. I just didn't want you chasing him around the rest of the summer."

"Who I date is my business," I told her.

"Not when you start dating boys who are already taken," Abby argued.

"I told you—"

"Why don't you do the smart thing and go back to Jeremy?" Abby cut in. "I hear he misses you."

"I'm going to do whatever is best for me," I said firmly, grateful that her friends were coming back.

"Give us all a break and stick with your guy," Abby repeated. I could tell she was accustomed to getting in the last word.

I hoped that they would leave right away, but

instead they hung around and ordered a medium sausage and onion pizza. It seemed as if they stayed forever, giggling and chattering. I took my break in Mr. Romano's back booth and read his copy of the *National Inquirer* while they ate their pizza. With any luck, Maria would get the honor of handling their check.

I stared at the pages full of Hollywood gossip, but I didn't really see the outrageous headlines. My own outrageous life overshadowed anything on the printed page. I hated the fact that so many people seemed to be spying on me—and interfering in my business. I certainly didn't intend to be told who I should and shouldn't date!

Fifteen minutes later, I folded up the paper and went back to the order counter. I rang up a young couple's tab and carefully counted out their change. My heart sank when I looked toward the front of the restaurant and saw that Abby and company were still munching on the final pieces of their pizza.

"Oh, waitress!" Abby called to me sweetly.

I rounded the counter, their bill in hand. "Thank you and come again soon," I said politely, setting the piece of paper by their empty pizza tin.

"I have a complaint," Abby said, her dark eyes gleaming with satisfaction. "There were onions on our pizza. We didn't order them."

"Yes, you did," I said.

"Mr. Romano! Mr. Romano!"

Much to my dismay, the boss immediately came bursting through the swinging kitchen door. "What is the trouble, ladies?" he asked, wiping his hands on his apron.

Abby whined and complained about the onions. I defended myself as best I could, trying not to get rude. I couldn't stand the thought of Abby getting away with this!

When Abby had finished complaining, there was a short silence. Mr. Romano looked from Abby to me to the table, rubbing his finger through his bushy gray moustache.

"She goofed, Mr. Romano," Abby repeated.

"What are you after, Abby, a free pizza?" Mr. Romano asked brusquely.

"Well, uh . . ." Abby gulped. She looked taken by surprise by his straightforward question. Obviously she had just figured I'd be chewed out in royal style—or better yet, fired on the spot.

"I am a very busy man," he continued, his sharp eyes pinned on Abby. "If the pizza was unsatisfactory, I will not charge you a cent."

Abby's voice shook a little, but she moved in for the kill anyway. "The waitress is the problem, not the food."

"Make up your mind!" Mr. Romano bellowed. "You either liked the pizza or you did not."

"It was good," Abby admitted. "It's just that

74

we didn't order onions on it, but Karen wrote them down anyway." Abby held up the check for him to see.

I clenched my fists in silent anger. I couldn't believe that even a spoiled brat like Abby would stoop so low to jeopardize my job.

"I could sympathize if you had sent the pizza back after tasting it," Mr. Romano said, "but you girls ate the entire thing!"

Abby blushed and stared at her manicured fingernails. He'd easily outsmarted her with a weapon she knew nothing about—common sense. "We'll pay," she surrendered, pushing back her chair to rise. She didn't look at me.

"Don't let that silly girl upset you," Mr. Romano comforted me gruffly after the threesome went marching out the door.

"I won't," I said with a sigh.

"You're doing a good job. It's hard on all of us being shorthanded. It looks as though I'm going to have to hire another person to keep up with business. Do you know a responsible kid like you who's looking for work?'"

"Not really," I replied, sorry that Mandy had rushed over to the dress shop yesterday. It would have been great working with her.

"I'll figure something out," Mr. Romano said, turning on his heel and returning to the kitchen.

My family was just sitting down to dinner when I arrived home shortly after six o'clock.

"You're just in time," Mom said, beckoning me into the kitchen. She was about to set dinner down in the center of the table: a big, steaming-hot pizza loaded with olives, mushrooms and pepperoni, and layered with a blanket of cheese.

I usually love pizza, but after smelling it all day, I felt like I wouldn't be able to eat it for weeks! "I think I'll pass on the pizza," I said, poking my head into the refrigerator in search of something safe like peanut butter and jelly.

"Don't tell me you overdosed on pizza at work," Mom scolded, suppressing a smile.

"Sort of," I said.

"You'd better not make a habit out of that, dear," she warned.

"Yeah, you don't want to get fat," Peter added, pulling a large slice of pizza onto his plate with relish.

I shot him an exasperated look as I made my sandwich. "I think I'll take this up to my room," I said, taking the glass of milk from my place at the table.

"But you can't run off until you've heard my wonderful news," Mom said excitedly.

"You won the lottery," Dad guessed.

"You found that fortune-teller's earring," Tiffany guessed.

"Oh, don't be silly." Mom laughed.

"You invited Rich Feldon to dinner," I joked dryly.

"Not even close. I set up driving lessons for you, Karen," Mom announced proudly.

That was great news! "How did you do it?" I asked.

"Marsha Bennett and I were chatting over coffee today about you children and—"

"I don't like the way you're looking at me, Mom," Peter said uncomfortably. "Karen is a good kid, but I don't want to teach her to drive."

"Simmer down and listen to the facts," Mom said. "Mark and Mandy apparently are having the same problem, so Marsha and I decided that the only sensible thing to do would be to trade sons for the lessons. Mark will teach Karen, and Peter will teach Mandy."

"That's a great idea, Mom," I said, as Peter choked on a mouthful of pizza.

"Don't trap me in the same vehicle with Mandy, Mom," Peter pleaded. "I'd go crazy in a confined space with her! She snaps her gum, fiddles constantly with the radio dial, and sings off-key to the music—whether she knows the words or not!"

"It's the only way," Mom stated in a no-nonsense tone. "Karen has no time to lose. Like you and Tiffany, she is trying to hold down a job. The very least this family can do is support her effort."

"Please, Peter," I coaxed, sitting down with my sandwich.

"We can't very well expect Mark to instruct Karen without paying back the courtesy to the Bennetts," Dad pointed out.

"No! Not in a million years," Peter argued stubbornly.

"Not in a million years," Mom agreed. "Tomorrow. Nine o'clock. Back alley. Be there."

Finally Peter relented. "You drive a hard bargain," he said, shaking his head.

"From now on, Pete, you can leave the driving to us," I said as I bit into my sandwich.

Chapter Six

"The most important lesson I can teach you about driving is to relax," Mark told me patiently. We were out in the back alley sitting in his orange Charger. I was in the driver's seat, testing the feel of the steering wheel.

"I'm hanging loose," I said. I closed my eyes for a moment, imagining that I was cruising down a wide elegant street in nearby Beverly Hills, weaving around BMWs and Ferraris with practiced ease. When I opened my eyes again, I was back in the alley with only one car in sight—Peter's maroon Camaro. It was moving jerkily ahead of us with Mandy at the wheel. I could see Peter's golden-brown head, the same shade as mine, swinging back and forth on the passenger side.

They had gotten off to a pretty good start. Mandy hadn't uttered one complaint when Peter shut off the radio and confiscated her gum—right as she was about to put it in her mouth! But somewhere between strapping on the seat belts and firing up the engine, things must've gone sour.

"Well, let's start our engine," Mark said.

"Look!" I exclaimed, pointing out the windshield at the Camaro. Mandy had swung open the driver's door and was climbing out of the car.

"You heartless jerk!" she cried, slamming the door shut. She stomped several yards back down the alley toward us and disappeared into the Bennett garage.

Peter too was on his feet in no time, circling his car like an Indian on the warpath. "This is a delicate piece of machinery!" he yelled. "You don't slam the doors or toy with the controls!" Mandy was no longer in sight, but Peter continued to shout in the direction of the Bennetts' garage.

"There seems to be a little misunderstanding brewing," Mark murmured, a trace of a smile on his lips.

Peter was now behind the wheel of his Camaro. He shifted the car into reverse and rolled back until he was parallel with Mark's Charger.

"There's pink bubble gum on my leather steering wheel cover!" Peter growled. He looked harassed to the limit. His hair was tousled over his forehead and his eyes were wild.

"But you took Mandy's gum away," I said, puzzled. "How could she have done any damage?"

Peter's face reddened to the color of a ripe tomato. "I did it myself!" he snapped furiously. "When I took her gum away, I guess it softened up between my fingers. When I leaned over to guide the wheel in her clumsy hands, the gooey stuff spread everywhere."

Mark's hearty laughter rang out in the warm summer air.

"Let's give it up, Mark," Peter suggested. "Hop in my car and we'll head for the beach."

"No way," Mark replied. "Your relationship with my sister has nothing to do with Karen's lessons."

"My *relationship!*" Peter gawked at his best friend. "With that menace?"

"If you don't mind, Pete, Karen and I would like to get on with our lesson." Mark's tone was calm and confident, the exact opposite of my brother's.

"You don't understand, Mark," Peter persisted. "You don't have to go through with the deal anymore if I don't. All we have to do is stick together."

"He's right, you know," I reluctantly agreed. I couldn't believe how close I'd come to finally

81

getting my lessons. But I didn't want to force Mark into anything.

"Our plans haven't changed, Karen," Mark assured me before turning back to Peter. "You handle your wheel problems and I'll handle mine. I promised to give Karen lessons, and I'm going to see them through."

"Have it your way," Peter grumbled, taking off down the alley.

"Don't tense up on me, now," Mark said when he turned back to me. His gray eyes were full of reassurance.

"I'll try not to," I said half-heartedly, wondering if Mark really wanted to go through with the lessons. Maybe he didn't actually mean I was a "wheel problem," but the way he put it made me feel sort of like a burden.

Mark explained all the different gears and controls on the dashboard while we were in the alley, then we switched places and he drove the Charger over to Fairmont High's parking lot to give us more maneuvering space. We spent over an hour there while he coached me on the basics. I drove back and forth across the blacktop, getting the feel of the brake and gas pedals without any interference from other vehicles.

"I guess we'd better stop for today," Mark said, glancing at his watch. "I'm due at work in a little while."

"I'm due at work in five minutes!" I realized

with dismay when I saw what time it was. "You don't mind dropping me off at Romano's, do you?"

"I do mind," Mark said flatly. He laughed as I stared at him in surprise. "I think you should drive yourself over there, Karen. After all, *you* are behind the wheel."

"Oh, I don't know . . ." I trailed off fearfully.

"You do have your learner's permit," Mark said. "It's only two blocks away."

"The Nook is right on Seventeenth Street, like the front of the school," I reminded him nervously.

"So what?"

"So, it's a very busy street, especially in the afternoon."

"We'll sneak up on old Mr. Romano from the rear," Mark proposed. "Like a tank in an old World War II movie."

"Very funny, Bennett. Very funny."

"Let's just not call each other names like Mandy and Peter do." Mark said it lightly, but his gray eyes were serious.

"We won't sink that low," I promised. Though I hadn't thought about it much, I already knew that Mark was a pretty sensitive guy. He and Peter had been the best of friends for years, but they were actually quite different.

I took the side streets to the Nook. My arms were shaking with every turn, and my foot was rarely off the brake. But I made it. And we were both in one piece.

"Good job," Mark praised, as I rolled between two yellow lines by the side of the building.

"Thanks." I shifted into park and shut off the engine, feeling rather pleased with myself. I turned to Mark and noticed all of a sudden that there was a dimple in the center of his square chin when he smiled. "I really appreciate this chance to practice behind the wheel," I ventured shyly, unsure about how he felt now that Peter had abandoned Mandy.

"It's sort of a practice run for me too," Mark revealed. He looked a bit shy himself. "I'd like to teach school someday, maybe coach basketball too. These lessons are my chance to see if I'm any good at giving instructions."

There certainly was a lot more to Mark than I'd realize, and it was nice getting to know him a little better. "Peter's never mentioned your plans," I said in surprise.

"Peter doesn't know about my plans," Mark said, his gray eyes wary now. "I'm afraid he might think they're dumb. His ambitions are a lot different from mine."

"I know. The last I heard, Peter wanted to be a movie director."

"Yeah." Mark sighed.

"Well, we know he's bossy enough!"

Mark nodded, and we laughed together. "I

guess I should be shoving off," he said. "Sid is very temperamental about employees who show up late."

"Sid sounds like quite a character," I said, curiosity getting the best of me. "I should drop by the liquidators sometime and see for myself."

"Aw, it's really pretty dull," Mark hedged, running a hand through his curly black hair.

I could tell he didn't like the idea much. I guess he thought I was crowding him. First the lessons, then the ride to the Nook, and now I was making plans to visit the place where he worked.

"I see Jeremy Miller's car is here," Mark said with a grimace.

"I'm not surprised," I said with a sigh. "This is his favorite hangout."

"You know, Peter would be really mad if he thought Jeremy was bothering you," Mark told me. He cast an annoyed look toward the Nook.

"I can handle things without Peter looking over my shoulder all the time," I answered.

"I guess you know what you're doing," Mark said without enthusiasm.

"Yes. Thanks again for the lesson, Mark." I reached into the back seat for my purse.

"We'll do it again soon," he promised, his eyes warming a bit.

"Karen!" Mr. Romano greeted me jovially as I entered the restaurant. "You got your license!"

"Not yet," I admitted reluctantly. "But I'm working on it."

"That's fine," he said, though he looked a trifle disappointed. "We can manage until you do. I hired another employee today who can make some of the deliveries."

"Who?" I asked. "Anyone I know?"

"Jeremy Miller," he announced, his round face beaming. "He spends so much time here anyway. I figured—well, who would know the Nook better?"

"Hi, Karen." Jeremy joined us. He was carrying a plastic tub full of dirty dishes. "I bused tables seven and eight," he informed Mr. Romano smoothly.

"Good work, son." Mr. Romano patted him on the back. "I like an employee who hustles without being told. Keep up the good work," he said, leaving us alone.

"Surprised to see me?" Jeremy asked. His suntanned face was full of excitement.

"I can't believe this," I said, definitely annoyed. "You've been hanging around the Nook forever, but you've never considered getting a job here."

"I want to be near you, Karen," Jeremy blurted out, setting his tub of dishes down on a nearby table. "I figured Mr. Romano would get steamed if I just hung around everyday taking you away from your chores. But if we're working together, he'll expect us to be talking all the time."

"I'm serious about this job, Jeremy," I told him firmly. "I want to keep up with Peter and Tiffany."

"I'm serious about working, too," he said sincerely. "But I'm also serious about proving that I'm your mystery man."

"So you know about that, huh?" I bit my lip nervously.

"Sure. You know, word gets around. *I* am the right one for you, Karen. It blows me away that you can't see it."

"I could never go back to the way things used to be, Jeremy. I will never follow you—or any other boy—around again. I've been making my own decisions lately and I'm proud of it."

Looking back on the past year, I could see that Jeremy had kept me under his spell right from the start. We had started going steady even before the Homecoming dance. By the time the Christmas Ball had rolled around, Jeremy was telling me what clothes to wear, what movies to watch, and what classes to take. By the Spring Formal, he was monopolizing all my time. I hardly even saw my own family! Finally, it had become too much. I liked Jeremy, but I needed time on my own, too!

"Things will be different this time," Jeremy promised. He sounded as if he meant it. "I won't make up a lot of rules or spoil your plans at home."

"I'll think about it, Jeremy," I relented. "If things go well for us at work, maybe."

"Could you do me one favor in the meantime?" he asked, twisting a lock of my hair around his finger. "Stop dating other guys like Rich Feldon and Mark Bennett."

"What!" I said, staring at him in surprise. "First of all, Rich will be back with Abby in no time, and Mark is just doing me a big favor by teaching me how to drive."

"But—"

"You just promised not to poke into my business," I said with a warning glance.

"Okay, okay."

"We'd better get to work," I said. Maria was swamped with customers.

"Right," Jeremy agreed, picking up his tub. "I can wait for you. We have the whole summer ahead of us."

I had to admit that having Jeremy at the Nook made things a lot easier. He was a hard worker, and the customers liked him—he had a way of making each one feel important. But I shouldn't have been surprised. I already knew firsthand that he had the knack for charming a person.

Mr. Romano gave me permission to sit in his

booth for my afternoon break. He joined me there with a mug of coffee and a cigar.

"I borrowed your newspaper," I said, looking up from the Entertainment section. "I hope it's all right."

"Help yourself," he invited. He sat across from me, puffing on his cigar. Smoke billowed around his head. "So what is new in the world today?"

"I don't know," I admitted with a sheepish grin. "I was just checking my horoscope."

Mr. Romano chuckled, his dark eyes shining with amusement. "What is in store for you?"

"It says here that a work project proceeds without a hitch."

"Sounds true. You're having a good day," Mr. Romano commented, puffing thoughtfully.

" 'Sudden developments will work in your favor,' " I continued.

"Things can happen pretty suddenly around here," Mr. Romano said, "especially to a waitress like you."

"And it says domestic arguments can be avoided if you use tact."

"That make any sense to you?" he asked.

"I'm not sure," I said with a shrug. But I had a feeling that it concerned Jeremy and my family. I could definitely avoid trouble by not telling my family that Jeremy was working at the Pizza Nook, too.

"Read mine," Mr. Romano requested, to my surprise.

"Okay. What's your sign?"

"Sign?"

"When is your birthday?"

"October twenty-fifth," he told me.

"That makes you a Scorpio," I said, skimming the horoscope column. "It says here that negotiations with foreigners should go well. Sounds pretty offbeat to me."

"Teenagers are like foreigners to me," Mr. Romano said deadpan.

I grinned. "It might mean that," I agreed before continuing. "It also says that property investments are favored."

"My brother-in-law was trying to sell me some property. I'll have to give that some thought. Oh, by the way, Karen, I want you to know that I'm trying to locate your fortune-teller, Xaviera. I put a notice on the bulletin board up front."

"That's great!" I said. I wanted nothing more than to get a second reading.

"I'm planning to introduce a new pizza in a few weeks, and I thought I could hire her to read palms or something. A gimmick to attract customers."

"Great idea, Mr. Romano. I—"

"Hi, Karen. Hi, Mr. Romano." My brother stood beside the booth looking down at us with a tentative smile. After the crazy way he had acted about the driving lessons in the morning, I couldn't believe he had the nerve to speak to me at all.

"Why hello, Peter," Mr. Romano greeted my brother warmly.

"Would it be okay if I talked to Karen for a minute?" Peter asked politely.

"Certainly," my boss replied. He ground out his cigar in the ashtray. "I have to get back to the kitchen anyway."

Peter slid into the spot Mr. Romano had left across from me. "You mad at me?" he asked, looking contrite.

"I could've lost my driving lessons because of you," I scolded. "And poor Mandy. I'll bet she's crushed!"

"I'm sorry I blew up at her," Peter apologized. "I don't know what got into me. For some crazy reason, Mandy lights my fuse faster than anybody else I know." Peter shook his head.

"Will you give the lessons another chance?" I asked.

"Yeah, yeah," Peter said, rolling his eyes. "I'll call her when I get home."

"I'm so glad that you changed your mind," I said gratefully. "Mandy and Mark have been such close friends for so long, I'd hate for anything to spoil it."

"Me too. But I really have to suffer at times like this to keep the friendship alive."

Suddenly Jeremy breezed by carrying a large pizza and a pitcher of soda. "Hi, Babe. How's it going, Peter?" He didn't wait for a response, but continued to a table near the window.

"What is *he* doing here, Karen?" Peter said angrily.

"He's working here now," I replied. "I'm not seeing him again. Not yet, anyway."

"He's not for you, Karen. Didn't that fortune-teller convince you of that?"

"According to my fortune, he could be my mystery match," I said defensively.

"She didn't mean him!"

"How do *you* know?"

Peter shrugged, looking frustrated. "He can't be the one, that's all."

"Well, I may have another chance to talk to Xaviera," I told him with a teasing grin.

"What?" Peter's mouth dropped open in surprise.

"Mr. Romano wants to hire her for a promotion deal. He put a notice on the bulletin board. He's sure someone must know her.

"Good luck to him," Peter said doubtfully. "Considering that she didn't succeed in steering you away from Jeremy Miller, I really doubt her powers are worth much."

"I should get back to work," I said, folding up the newspaper.

Suddenly Peter laughed. "Boy, if Mom and Dad find out about Jeremy working here—pow!"

I rapped him in the stomach with the folded paper. "If Mom and Dad find out that you chewed Mandy out this morning and chased her out of the car—pow!"

Peter threw up his palms in defeat. "I do believe we can strike up an agreement here," he said.

"I kind of figured we could," I said with a sly smile.

Chapter Seven

Mark gave me a driving lesson every day for the next two weeks. By the following Saturday, I was pretty confident behind the wheel. Peter had patched things up with Mandy as he had promised, and they too spent a lot of time over at the high school parking lot in Peter's Camaro.

To pay the guys back for their efforts, Mandy and I treated them to a pizza at the Nook on Saturday night.

"I suppose you get an employee's discount on this meal, Sis," Peter said, as he piled several pieces of pizza on his plate.

I was refilling everyone's glass with root beer and paused to glare at him. "I certainly do not!"

"We're picking up the tab ourselves," Mandy chimed in proudly. "Now that Karen and I are wage earners, we can afford it."

"I could easily get used to being taken out this way," Mark said with a wink.

"You guys show us how things work under the hood next week, and we'll take you out again," I promised, tipping my glass of root beer to my lips.

"Hey, Karen," Peter said excitedly, "if you're really interested in engines, I have a great idea."

"What?" I demanded suspiciously. I never trusted that smirk of his.

"Listen up," he said, his voice dropping to a whisper. "Bill Kennedy walked in a few minutes ago. He's sitting behind you near the jukebox."

"So?" I asked in confusion, dabbing my mouth with a napkin.

"So, dummy, maybe *he's* your mystery match," he said, patting me on the back as if I were a child.

"This is your chance to follow up on another guy," he urged. He paused to send Jeremy—who was clearing a table across the room—the evil eye.

"Leave it alone, Pete," Mark suggested—to my surprise.

Peter shot Mark a puzzled glance. "That fortune-teller mentioned wheels, and nobody is more into wheels than Bill Kennedy. And since when do you care about this mystery, anyhow?" he added curiously.

To his obvious discomfort, Mark found all three of us staring at him. "I just don't want Karen to get all worked up about anything when she's on the verge of taking her driver's exam," he said as he reached for another slice of pizza. "I didn't want you to worry about it all weekend, Karen, but I made an appointment for your exam for next Tuesday at four o'clock. I don't want to fail with my first pupil," he added, his gray eyes twinkling.

"I'll try to keep my cool about everything," I promised.

"So, how is the deluxe pizza?" Mr. Romano was standing next to our table.

"Great!" we assured him in unison.

"It looks as if you're going to have another driver very soon," Peter told him proudly. "Karen is set to take the driver's test next Tuesday afternoon."

"Well, well," Mr. Romano boomed with pleasure. "That is wonderful news. I wish my other business dealing today had worked out just as well," he added with a flicker of disappointment.

"What happened?" Peter asked. "Did Jeremy Miller drop a pizza on the floor and serve it anyway?"

"Peter!" I said sharply. Once again, he'd gone too far. To add to my discomfort, Jeremy must have heard his name mentioned. He flashed us an annoyed look.

Mr. Romano let the gibe pass without comment. "My promotion plans look pretty bleak. I talked to that fortune-teller, Xaviera, today, and she—"

"You really talked to her?" I jumped out of my cracked vinyl chair and confronted my boss. "Who is she? Is she coming?"

"She isn't coming," Mr. Romano replied regretfully. "I don't know much else. She said her schedule is too hectic these days to allow for personal appearances."

"But she came to my birthday party," I said, wondering why she had made an exception in my case.

"I tried my best to find out who had hired her for your party, but she sidestepped me quite cleverly," he said, stroking his chin thoughtfully.

"Well, *someone* knows her," I said. "Someone saw your notice on the bulletin board by the door and relayed the message to her."

"Most likely," Mr. Romano agreed. "But it's possible that she saw the ad herself. All sorts of people come in and out of this place. For instance, your parents stopped by one night shortly after you left, Karen."

My stomach was churning. So my folks probably knew about Jeremy working at the Nook!

"It seems like everybody who comes in here stops to read that bulletin board," Mr. Romano continued. "Jeremy checks it every day. And you Bennett kids were looking something over earlier this week," he recalled, focusing on Mark and Mandy.

"Mom is looking for a used exercise bike," Mark said hastily.

"What's the difference if you find Xaviera or not?" Peter cut in. "It seems as though all the guidance in the world won't steer you away from Jeremy Miller. Why bother to track down this woman?"

Now Jeremy was walking toward us. He must have heard his name mentioned again. "I'm sick of everybody telling Karen what to do!" he complained. His handsome face was angry.

"Sure you are, Miller," Peter snapped. "You told her what to do the whole time you dated her, and now you're mad because she wised up and dumped you!"

"I'm that mystery guy she's looking for," Jeremy insisted, jabbing his thumb at his chest. "And she's going to figure it out one of these days!"

I'm sure my face was as red as the checked vinyl tablecloths in the Nook. "Please stop it, you two," I pleaded.

"Yes," Mr. Romano reprimanded. "This is a place of business. Jeremy, please get back to your duties!"

"Yes, sir." Jeremy reluctantly headed for the back counter.

"I'm sorry, Mr. Romano," I apologized, feeling humiliated. He shrugged and headed back to the kitchen.

"Peter, you are terrible," I muttered after my boss was out of earshot.

"You need someone to look after you, Karen," Peter grumbled.

"Seems to me that you're trying to control my life just as much as Jeremy ever did," I said coolly.

I couldn't eat another bite, so Peter polished off my last slice of pizza. No one had much to say after that. Mandy made a couple of attempts to start a conversation, but Mark was completely silent, and Peter and I were too busy glaring at each other to join in. What had started out as a wonderful time had turned into a terrible flop. And it wasn't over. I still had to face my parents and explain why Jeremy was working with me at the Nook.

Mom was sitting in the kitchen folding laundry when Peter and I got home. "How was your evening?" she asked, adding a neatly folded sheet to a stack of linens on the round oak table.

"Okay," Peter said, swinging open the refrigerator door. "Anything to eat in here?" he asked, dipping his head out of sight behind the door.

"You can't be hungry!" I exclaimed, dropping into a chair across from Mom. "We just ate."

He straightened up to look at us. "I'm a growing boy," he said. Then he disappeared from sight again.

"Don't you ever think about anything but your stomach?" Mom scolded. But her blue eyes were glowing with amusement.

"Aw, Mom." Peter emerged with an apple and a small carton of fruit juice. "I think I'll take these up to my room," he said, ruffling Mom's short brown hair as he passed the table. "I can't stand to watch tearful confessions. They kill my appetite."

"What do you mean, Peter?" Mom asked him.

Peter waved his free hand and walked out without answering, so naturally Mom turned to me.

I took an unsteady breath. "I know that you probably know about Jeremy working at the Pizza Nook," I blurted out in a rush of words.

"Oh, so you heard that we had stopped by," Mom said, handing me a fluffy peach towel to fold.

"Yes, Mr. Romano told me." I busily smoothed out the towel, grateful that my nervous hands had a task.

"I'm not surprised you didn't mention it," Mom said. She sounded more disappointed than annoyed. "Can't that boy give you a moment to yourself?"

"There wasn't anything I could do about it," I explained. "On my second day of work Mr. Romano announced that he'd hired Jeremy. I figured you'd be mad, and I didn't mention it because I was just trying to avoid a hassle—at least for a little while. . . ."

"At least until you decide whether Jeremy is your mystery match," Mom said.

My self-conscious expression must have given me away immediately. Mom made a clucking sound as she watched my face.

"I want you to know I realize that Jeremy made too many demands on me before," I said quickly. "I'm not going off the deep end over him again. If we do get back together, it will be a lot different this time."

"I trust you to make your own decisions," Mom said, though she still sounded hesitant.

"But what?" I urged.

"But I hoped this fortune thing would spark your imagination—send you off in other directions."

Suddenly I wondered if Mom *had* arranged for Xaviera to appear at my party after all. "Which fortune do you mean," I asked with a smile, "your's or Xaviera's genuine one?"

Mom's expression was impossible to read. "It doesn't matter, really. As far as I'm concerned, *you* have more power over your future than either a crystal ball or an upside-down fishbowl."

I shook my head in disbelief as Mom headed out of the room with a stack of folded laundry. It didn't seem as if I'd ever solve the mystery of Xaviera's appearance!

Chapter Eight

I was the only one in the family who didn't have plans for Sunday night. Mom and Dad were taking Joy to an ice show downtown. Tiffany had a date with a fellow counselor from the day camp. And Peter, the lucky guy, was going to a beach party sponsored by the class that had just graduated from Fairmont High.

Everyone was busy that afternoon, getting ready for their activities. I, on the other hand, had nothing better to do than sit up in my room on the windowseat and gaze down at the backyard below. I didn't feel like reading or watching a movie, and Mandy was busy. There really wasn't any interesting action outside, unless you counted Peter and Mark washing the Camaro. They were clowning around in the alley with the garden hose, a bucket of sudsy water, and a couple of giant sponges.

I sighed and hugged my giant teddy bear. Here I was, on a gorgeous summer day, and I was stuck all alone in my room hugging Winnie the Pooh. There had to be more to life—like a little romance.

"Hey, mopey." Tiffany poked her head full of curlers into my room. "Peter wants to talk to you."

"What does he want?" I asked dully, tossing my bear aside.

Tiffany shrugged. "I don't know. He just asked me to send you outside."

"Maybe he wants me to vacuum the interior of his car," I said irritably.

"Preparing for that party at Pine Lake is all he cares about," Tiffany confided with a huge grin. "He used some of my conditioner on his hair this morning, and he even borrowed one of Dad's designer shirts to wear over his swim trunks."

"What's all the fuss about?" I said, glancing down at the guys, who were now buffing the Camaro's windshield to a perfect shine.

"Our dear brother plans to find a hot date on the beach, somewhere between the volleyball net and the bonfire," Tiffany replied with a hoot. "What a dreamer."

"He'd have better luck with girls if he'd keep quiet for ten seconds," I added. Suddenly Peter spotted me in the window and beckoned. "Guess

I'll go see what he's so antsy about," I said. "Maybe he wants some advice on how to talk to a girl without making her mad."

"Come here, kid!" Peter called as I walked across the lawn. "Hurry up!"

"What's up?" I asked suspiciously, leaning against the back fender of the Camaro beside Mark.

"I have a real treat for you," Peter said, reaching into the back pocket of his jeans.

"You're going to give me some money?" I guessed doubtfully.

"Yeah, right!" Peter scoffed. He opened his wallet and began to flip through the plastic-covered photograph-holders. "Ah, here she is," he said.

"You're giving her a photo of someone?" Mark asked, looking puzzled. He obviously wasn't in on Peter's latest scheme, for which I was grateful.

Peter shook his head and pulled out two green tickets. "A customer at Sid's gave me two passes to the Auto Show today at the Civic Center."

"But we're going to the beach," Mark protested.

"True, buddy. These tickets are for Karen."

"What are you talking about," I said, totally confused. "You guys are the car freaks, not me."

"But Bill Kennedy is," Peter pointed out patiently, as if he were trying to reason with an idiot.

"Bill Kennedy!" I cried. "If you told him I'd go out with him, I'll kill you, Peter Daly!"

"That was really low," Mark added.

The grin on Peter's face didn't wave a bit. "There's only one way to find your mystery man, and that is to follow up on all the possibilities."

"How dare you organize a date without asking me first!"

"I don't believe you, Pete," Mark broke in. "Here comes Bill now."

I followed Mark's gaze down the alley and spotted Bill's gangly form loping down the alley. I whirled toward Peter. "Tell me *exactly* what you said to Bill."

"I called him this morning and told him that if he dropped by about five o'clock, he'd have a chance to go to the Auto Show for free."

"You didn't mention my name?" I asked hopefully, my brain already turning over the possibilities.

Peter shook his head. "That's the beauty of this plan. I lured him over here with the perfect bait: a room full of cars. He's trapped, whether he likes it or not."

Mark suddenly flashed me a knowing smile, and I realized he understood my predicament. Suddenly I got a great idea.

"As far as Bill knows, he could be going to the show with you, Peter," I began.

"Heck no! He . . ." Peter's voice trailed off as he realized that I was right.

"Hi!" Bill greeted us, his freckled face brimming with excitement. "Is everyone going to the show?" he asked eagerly.

"No," I murmured, not very regretfully. "Peter only has two tickets."

Peter opened his mouth to speak, but Mark beat him to it. "Karen, as long as Peter's tied up, maybe you'd like to go to the beach party with me tonight."

"Sure, that would be super." My tone was grateful and surprised, but Bill didn't appear to notice.

"But—but—" Peter stuttered.

"It's all settled then," Mark said firmly, slapping my brother heartily on the back.

Bill wasted no time in climbing into the Camaro. "You keep this buggy in great shape, Peter," he said admiringly, rolling down the window.

"Yeah, yeah," Peter grumbled. "I'll be right back, Bill." He picked up the bucket and sponges and beckoned for us to follow him into the garage. "You rats!" he accused indignantly as soon as we were inside.

"You just outwitted yourself," I shot back with satisfaction. It was a rare occasion when I got the better of my brother. I had to admit I was enjoying it.

"So what if you have to suffer a little?" Mark said with a laugh. "It was *your* plan."

"But you can't go to that beach party, Karen," Peter objected. "It's only for our class."

"And their dates," Mark corrected, his gray eyes full of mischief.

"Come on, Karen. Go with Bill," Peter coaxed.

"No!" I practically shouted.

"Okay," Peter said with a long-suffering sigh. "But I'll be at the beach later—minus Mr. Mechanic."

"Take your time, buddy," Mark replied. "We can manage without you."

Peter looked stunned. "But what will the two of you *talk* about all by yourselves? You'd better take Mandy and her automatic jaw along to keep the conversation moving."

"Mandy is working until six o'clock," I informed him coldly. "And I'm capable of carrying on a conversation on my own."

"Just don't go over there and give our family a bad name, kid," Peter threw over his shoulder as he left the garage.

"I know how to handle myself," I tossed back defiantly, though I was not so sure. There seemed to be a million-mile gap between the sophomores and seniors during the school year. I doubted that summer vacation changed things much.

"Let's meet at my car in about two hours," Mark suggested, looking at his watch. "It'll be nearly seven o'clock by then and the party should be going strong."

"I appreciate what you did, Mark." A blush

warmed my face and I avoided his steady gaze. "I mean, getting me out of that jam with Bill Kennedy. But I don't expect you to, you know, really take me along to the beach or anything. . . ."

"You do want to go with me, don't you, Karen?" Mark's voice sounded anxious.

"But what will all the kids say?" I blurted out nervously. "I don't want to spoil your—uh—love life." I was beet red by now.

Mark laughed, causing me to suffer all the more.

I didn't think that was so funny. Mark had quite a reputation for dating some of the prettiest senior girls in the school, all of whom were far more sophisticated than I ever could be.

"We've always spent a lot of time together, Karen," Mark pointed out.

"But that was different," I protested, wandering over to my dad's work bench. I picked up a hammer and tapped it lightly on the wood. "Peter and Mandy have always been along. We've always been a foursome."

"We've been alone during our driving lessons. So what if we're together at a party?" Mark shoved his hands into the pockets of his jeans. "Everyone knows we're friends. I don't think we're going to blow anyone away."

"Okay," I gave in with a sigh of relief. "I'm convinced."

"I've never had to beg a girl to go out with me

108

before," Mark grumbled good-naturedly. "And considering that I was one of the guys at your birthday party, *I* could even be your mystery match."

Before I could respond, Mark disappeared out the large double door.

I thought about Mark's words as I was preparing for our date later that afternoon. He had to be joking about being a mystery match candidate, I decided as I slipped an oversize T-shirt over my red racer style swimsuit.

Or was he? I stared at my reflection in the dresser mirror and noticed that my eyes seemed a darker green than usual. Surely Mark didn't care about me in a romantic way. Not after all the years of seeing me in pigtails, with grass-stained knees and grubby clothes. Mark knew of nearly every fight I'd ever had with my folks, and every time I'd fallen off my bicycle. He knew too many of my embarrassing secrets to fall in love with me.

I shook my head forcefully, causing my hair to fall around my face like a brown curtain. It couldn't be true. Mark only fell for pretty girls with turned-up noses and high voices. Girls whom he hadn't watched suffer through the awkward stages of pre-adolescence. After all, once you've seen a girl in her flannel pajamas, there's not a whole lot left to dream about.

The sun was setting over Pine Lake as we pulled into the parking lot in Mark's car later that evening. The sky was a beautiful shade of lavender and pink, and the water reflected the sun's last rays, making the waves ripple gold in the distance.

"Looks like a great party," Mark observed as we got out of the car. He tilted the seat forward and removed his cooler and beach blanket from the back.

"Yeah, great," I agreed uncertainly. I slung my beach bag over my shoulder and stood watching the action in front of us. A volleyball net was set up haphazardly in the sand and a rowdy game was going on. There were the makings of a bonfire in a pile near the shoreline and, of course, there were plenty of kids in the water, splashing and shouting at each other.

Mark was suddenly at my side, his free arm draped casually around my shoulders. My heart fluttered a bit at his nearness. *This is good old Mark, I reminded myself. Let's not get carried away, Daly.* That fact didn't stop the fluttering, though. Ever since our driving lessons had begun, I couldn't help but notice that my perception of Mark had been changing. I was starting to see him more as a nice, gorgeous guy than just the boy next door. He certainly looked great right then in his brown tank shirt and tan and red swim trunks. But could he possibly be my mystery match? *No way,* I thought. I couldn't imagine a smooth guy like Mark, about to enter college, as being madly in love with me.

110

"Ready to hit the beach?" Mark asked, his gray eyes dancing with mischief.

"I don't know," I admitted uneasily. Would all action stop when we joined the crowd? I wondered. Would the kids all want to know why we were out together?

"Loosen up," Mark whispered in my ear. "Seniors don't bite." He clasped my hand and pulled me along behind him through the sand.

To my relief, no one made a mad rush at us to demand an explanation for our twosome. The only person who commented at all was Judy Dennison, one of Mark's regular dates from the past school year. She was exactly the kind of girl I'd always pictured as the type for Mark: blond and curvaceous, with a dimple centered in each cheek.

"Well, hello, stranger," she said, her round brown eyes gazing up at Mark. She looked wonderful in a shiny purple bikini and lacy coverup. Suddenly my red suit and T-shirt seemed childish. I stood silently beside Mark, awkwardly jamming my toe into the sand.

"Hi, Judy," Mark said, keeping his eyes on the lake. "Karen and I were just going for a swim."

"I've been waiting all summer for you to call me," Judy said with a pout. "And now you show up today with your little neighbor."

Mark reddened a bit. "I've been real busy at

Sid's. Summer hours and all that. Come on, Karen," he said, pulling off his T-shirt. "Talk to you later, Judy," he called over his shoulder as we headed for the water. But he didn't mean it, I could tell.

I forgot my fears as we blended in with the crowd. After a swim and an intense volleyball game, it seemed natural to sit down on a beach blanket near the bonfire with Mark and roast hot dogs and marshmallows.

Someone had brought a large tape player and a bunch of cassettes along. We happily ate our hot dogs to the music of the Beach Boys, Madonna, and U-2.

"Why does everything taste better when it's cooked outside?" Mark asked me over the din of the music.

His question startled me. I had been staring at his nicely-shaped profile, illuminated by the warm yellow glow of the fire. "What?" I asked sheepishly. Mark quickly realized that I'd been watching him. Our eyes locked and we gazed at each other for a long, wonderful moment. I knew then that Mark wanted to kiss me. The message was unmistakable in his tender expression. I tingled from head to toe as Mark's face moved close to mine. What would it be like? Was Mark the boy for me? These questions raced through my mind as his hand pressed against my back.

"Wow! What a bash!" Peter's voice cut like a sharp knife through the cool summer night. I looked up to find my brother and Mandy hovering over us like pesky flies.

"What are the two of you *doing*?" Mandy demanded, plopping down onto our blanket.

"Nothing special," I said shortly, staring into the fire.

"You really had your heads together over something," Peter put in, squatting down on the sand beside Mark.

"Not really," Mark said firmly. "How was the auto show?"

"It was okay," Peter grumbled. "The cars were super, but Bill was sort of a jerk. He insisted on inspecting every dashboard and kicking every tire. I probably wouldn't have minded ordinarily, but I really wanted to get to this beach party."

"It was nice of you to bring Mandy along," I said, a bit surprised.

"He didn't intend to," Mandy informed me, casting Peter a cold look. "Mom told me you were with Mark, so I tracked Peter down in the alley before he could get away."

Peter shook his head in disgust. "One chance to prowl for women on the beach and we end up stuck with our sisters. Tough break."

"It's your own fault," I reminded him. "You called Bill Kennedy and set up that date."

"Yeah, yeah." Peter raised his palms in surrender.

"I'm hungry," Mandy complained, sniffing the appetizing smell of roasting hot dogs in the air.

"There's plenty of stuff in my cooler," Mark invited with a resigned sigh.

Peter and Mandy soon polished off the rest of Mark's food, bickering back and forth about how to roast the perfect marshmallow.

Mark and I sat side by side for the rest of the evening, but the spell between us was broken. Maybe I'd been mistaken about Mark's feelings anyway. The bonfire had probably brought out romantic feelings in him temporarily and he'd impulsively decided to kiss me. Mark could have practically any girl he wanted. It seemed impossible that he could be in love with me from afar.

Chapter Nine

My driver's test was in the back of my mind all day Tuesday. I couldn't really concentrate on anything else, and I messed up whatever I put my hands on. I drove everybody who came near me crazy and began to wonder if I'd have a friend left on earth by the time my four o'clock appointment at the Driver's Exam Bureau rolled around.

"Karen!" Mom cried in alarm. She came rushing into the kitchen, waving her arms. "Are you ironing that shirt or baking it?"

"Oops!" I gasped and lifted the iron off Peter's green-and-white-striped shirt. The iron steamed and sputtered in protest in my hand, and Mom steamed and sputtered in protest across the ironing board.

"It's only ten o'clock in the morning. You've been causing havoc since sunrise!" she scolded.

"I only got up early to make Dad's breakfast because I couldn't sleep," I explained matter-of-factly.

"Yes, dear, but you're completely distracted by that test. Sprinkling red pepper instead of cinnamon on your father's cream of wheat got him off to a very grumpy start."

"You could hardly taste it—"

"Then you sucked Tiffany's birthstone ring up into the vacuum cleaner."

"It's not my fault she left it lying on the floor. And besides, I dug it out of the dust bag myself!"

"Yes, but you left a trail of vacuum dust all along the hallway upstairs. I had to clean the floor with a sponge mop."

"Oh." I flashed her an apologetic look. "I guess I didn't look back to see if I was dropping anything. But they were all accidents, Mom," I said as she gingerly pulled the iron from my tight grasp. "I can't help it. My horoscope in this morning's paper says catastrophes are looming ahead today, and that I must be on the lookout for fate's heavy hand. And today's my *driving* test!"

"There is nothing mystical about your behavior," Mom insisted, running the iron over the unevenly pressed shirt. "You're totally wound up over that test. Perhaps if you forget all about fate, and try to control your shaky nerves with logic, you won't burn the pizza place down this afternoon."

"Mr. Romano has lots of faith in me," I informed her with dignity. "He's assigning me to the kitchen today."

"You'll be using that big oven of his?" Mom looked a little worried. "In your frame of mind today?"

"Of course," I replied proudly. Mr. Romano knows I know what I'm doing."

"Hmmm" was all Mom said. But a faint smile was tugging at the corners of her mouth.

A rap on the back screen interrupted us.

"Hello, Mark," Mom said cheerily. "Come in and join us."

The screen door creaked as Mark walked in. His curly black hair looked a little windblown, but his gray eyes were full of energy. "You look pretty today, Karen," he said, sitting down at the table with the easy familiarity of a next-door neighbor.

"Thanks," I said, busily rearranging the napkins in the holder on the table. I hadn't seen Mark since the party, and I was a little self-conscious about our brush with romance.

"Karen has been making some absent-minded mistakes today. She's trying to blame it on her horoscope," Mom said. "But I know what the real reason is." She pointed to the fruit bowl on the table. "Have something to eat, Mark. You look hungry."

"Thanks." Mark reached for the only apple tucked between the bananas and oranges in the bowl.

"Mom thinks I'm nervous about the driver's test today, but I'm feeling really cool about it," I told him as confidently as I could.

A grin spread over Mark's face as he munched on the apple. "I'm a little nervous about the test myself," He admitted ruefully. "I cut part of your front lawn before I realized I'd crossed the property line!"

"Mr. Daly will be very pleased to hear it," Mom chuckled. "Perhaps you'd like to go back out there for a while in your preoccupied state!"

Mark laughed. "No, I'll let Peter have the honor of finishing up your grass. I still have our backyard to take care of."

"I suppose it's possible that I might be a little on edge about the test," I admitted. "But I guess it's kind of silly since the lessons went so well."

"Yes," Mom agreed. She set the iron down and lifted the shirt off the board. "We're so grateful that you kids worked it out among yourselves."

"Mark did a great job," I praised, noticing how muscular his arms were in his T-shirt. He was smart and strong as well. He always seemed capable of handling any problem. It was funny how much more I'd been seeing in Mark since the lessons began.

"Well, I should get back to work," he said, rising from the table to toss his apple core into the waste basket. "I just stopped by to firm up our plans, Karen. I'll meet you at the exam bureau at three-thirty. That will give you plenty of time to fill out all the papers."

"I'll be there," I promised. "No matter how many catastrophes I brew up this afternoon."

Mom turned to me after Mark disappeared down the back steps. "Why is Mark so worried about your exam?" she asked. "Peter is taking Mandy down to the bureau tomorrow, and *he* doesn't seem overly concerned."

"Mark wants to be a teacher and coach after he graduates from college," I said. "It means a lot to him to see me through these lessons."

"I see," Mom said. "He's testing his teaching skills on you."

"Right," I said with a nervous sigh. "I hope I don't let either one of us down."

"If I were you, I'd forget about your horoscope and pay attention to what you're doing at the Nook today," Mom advised. "If you can't stand the heat, get out of the kitchen."

"Too many cooks spoil the broth," I retorted with a laugh.

*   *   *

"You're going to be back here in the kitchen?" Jeremy demanded. "All afternoon?"

We were standing face-to-face across the long stainless steel table in Mr. Romano's spotless kitchen. The Nook was about to open, and I had come in early to learn pizza preparation Anthony Romano-style. The table was covered with prepared pizza dough, a large kettle of zesty sauce cooked with the secret family recipe, and assorted toppings in plastic tubs.

"I'll be in here all afternoon," I confirmed, smoothing the front of my huge white apron. All the aprons were sized for the round shapes of Mrs. Romano and her daughter Maria, and I'd had to tuck and tie the billowing garment around myself the best I could.

"You look like a deflated Pillsbury dough boy in that thing," Jeremy teased, his face alive with mischief. Suddenly a memory of all the good times we had had during the school year flooded back.

"I'm going to miss you out front," Jeremy admitted, leaning over the table until his clear blue eyes were inches from mine. "I miss you all the time, really," he added.

"It wasn't working anymore," I reminded both of us, as some sad memories joined the happy ones in my mind.

"I told you I'm willing to change," Jeremy

insisted softly. His face was still only inches away from mine.

"No kissing in my kitchen!" Mr. Romano boomed, suddenly appearing through the swinging door leading to the dining area.

"Oh!" I almost died of embarrassment. A red-hot blush rose to my face as I jumped back away from the table and Jeremy.

"Sorry, Mr. Romano," Jeremy said self-consciously, running a hand through his dark blond hair. "I guess I should get back out on the floor."

The boss nodded his head firmly. "Karen is going to be leaving early today, so we'll all have to work hard and be on our toes."

"Where are you going?" Jeremy asked, instantly interested.

Mr. Romano cut in before I could respond. "She is leaving at three-fifteen. She has some plans with Mark Bennett that we needn't discuss with a dining room full of customers waiting to be served!"

"But—"

"Never mind, young man!" Mr. Romano growled impatiently, pushing Jeremy out through the swinging door. "I have an appointment this morning. I expect you to be Maria's right-hand man."

I got busy quickly, ladling the boss's thick tomato sauce on the prepared circles of dough.

I tried to keep Mom's advice in mind about staying alert and ignoring my horoscope.

"This pizza has bacon on it, Karen," Maria told me through the order window an hour later. Her round face held apology and irritation at the same time. "I know we're at the height of the lunch hour, but you must be careful!"

I picked up the guest check on the window ledge beside the pizza. "This pizza is for table one, not table seven," I said, pointing to the figure on the slip of paper. "Jeremy took the wrong pizza to a table in his station."

"I'm sorry," Maria said, looking frustrated. "Jeremy just isn't himself today. He's been mixing up the soda orders too—and he broke three glasses while he was busing the tables."

"Slippery fingers?" I asked, walking over to the oven to remove freshly baked pizzas with a large paddle-like spatula.

"Not if you ask me," Maria muttered. "He tosses the dishes into his tub as if they're rubber. Dad won't put up with that for long."

"Talking about me?" Jeremy asked, joining Maria at the order window.

"I'm trying to straighten out the pizza orders!" Maria told him angrily as she walked away.

"I swear she'd make a great drill sergeant," Jeremy said.

"She has a lot of responsibility on her shoulders today," I said, glancing at the clock.

"Every time I come back here you're looking at the clock," Jeremy complained. "Thinking about your date with Mark Bennett?"

"Jeremy, it's really none of your business, is it?" I reminded him. "Besides—"

"Never mind, Karen," He cut in sulkily. "Never mind."

I set three pizzas on the ledge of the window. "Please be careful with these orders, Jeremy. You're making both of us look bad."

"I know what's good for both of us, Karen, but you just can't see it." Before I could respond, he stalked away.

I spent my lunch break in the small park across from the high school. I had a chicken sandwich and carton of juice that I had brought along from home, and I sat contentedly in the sunshine enjoying the fresh July air. It was a relief to get away from the pressure of work—and the pressure Jeremy was putting on me to take him back.

Mr. Romano was back and hard at work when I returned to the Nook. "Come here, Karen," he called, beckoning me to the center of the black-and-white tiled floor. "A group of secretaries from the Court House are coming to celebrate a promotion or something," he explained. "Could you help me arrange these tables and chairs in one long row?"

"Sure," I said, pitching in to help him.

"Maria told me what a fine job you did on the pizzas while I was away," Mr. Romano said gruffly.

"I tried to keep up the best I could," I replied. I was glowing inside.

"She said no one's ever arranged the toppings so artistically," he said with a chuckle. "They were like clocks. Pepperoni numbers, mushroom minute hands, all on a mozzarella background."

"I didn't mean to do that," I gasped.

Mr. Romano went behind the counter and returned with some red-and-white checkered tablecloths. "She didn't mind at all. By the way, I am impressed with your interest in the driver's exam this afternoon," he said. "It shows initiative."

I unfolded the tablecloths and spread them neatly on the scarred wooden tables, my spirits brightening a little. Things weren't going so badly after all. If I just kept my head until three-fifteen, I'd be on my way to the exam feeling calm and cool.

The secretaries had ordered their pizzas in advance, so I headed for the kitchen to prepare them. I was surprised to find Jeremy in the kitchen folding up a stepstool in the corner of the room near the sink.

"What are you doing?" I asked curiously.

He jumped a little. "Nothing!" he said. He cleared his throat and tugged at the neck of his red Nook T-shirt. "I've been on my lunch break, too."

"Oh," I said uncomfortably. "I hope you're not mad at me about this morning—"

"No!" he exclaimed. "No, Karen. I'm just eager for you to see that I'm the guy for you." He sighed and picked up a plastic tub from beside the sink. "Talk to you later."

I got busy with the pizzas and forgot about the clock and Jeremy. The food was all ready when the secretaries arrived. Mr. Romano proudly served them himself.

The large round clock on the wall read nearly three o'clock, so I began cleaning up the kitchen counter. Maria startled me moments later when she poked her head through the order window. "You have a phone call on line two, Karen," she said.

I picked up the extension hanging on the kitchen wall. "This is Karen," I said uncertainly. I'd never received a call at work before. Was something wrong at home?

"This is Mark, Karen. What's going on?"

"Not much. I—"

"Karen, how could you mess up our plans?

125

You were going to leave work at three-fifteen and meet me at the exam bureau at three-thirty."

"But it's only going on three o'clock!" I protested, yanking off my apron as we spoke.

"No, it's four o'clock! I've been at the bureau for more than half an hour!"

"*What*?" I gasped. "I just checked the clock. I—I don't understand how this could have happened," I said in a shaky voice.

"I don't either," Mark fired back. "I took off work to make this appointment. I had to promise Sid I'd work next Saturday to make up for it."

"I'm sorry! It's not my fault, Mark!" I said. "I've been watching the clock most of the day. It must be running slow—"

"If you don't care, I can't make you care!" he snapped.

Suddenly the dial tone buzzed in my ear.

"What's wrong?" Mr. Romano asked, pushing open the swinging door.

I sniffed and hung up the telephone. "What time is it?"

"Four o'clock." He glanced at his watch, then at the clock on the wall. "My clock is broken." Suddenly a frown crossed his large-featured face. "You missed your exam, Karen! It is all my fault."

Maria joined us in the kitchen. "What's wrong?"

Tears burned my eyes as Mr. Romano told her about the clock.

"This is very weird," Maria murmured. Her voice was suspicious. "I caught Jeremy up on the stepstool earlier fiddling with the clock. I asked him what he was doing, and he claimed that it was running a few minutes behind."

"Oh, no," I groaned. I remembered that he had been folding up the stepstool when I returned from lunch.

"He sounded sincere, so I didn't question it. I was busy with customers, and it didn't seem important."

"He always sounds sincere," I said. "No one knows that better than I do!"

"I will take care of that young man," Mr. Romano vowed. His eyes were narrowed to slits.

"Let me have him first!" I said. I marched out to the dining area before he could answer.

Jeremy knew what was coming. He stopped clearing a booth and followed me out to the sidewalk.

"How could you do it, Jeremy?" I demanded angrily against the hum of the heavy traffic.

"I had to do something," he said. "You don't belong with Bennett. I couldn't let you meet him!"

"I was supposed to take my driver's exam today!" I cried. My heart was pumping furiously. "Mark was seeing my lessons through to the end."

"Well, why didn't you just say so?" he asked, looking sheepish.

"Because I didn't have to!" I returned angrily. "You have no right to poke into my business. You promised you weren't going to do that anymore!"

"But this was different," he insisted. "I couldn't let you take off with somebody else."

"You're trying to take charge of my life again, just the way you did before, Jeremy," I said. "You'll never change."

"You're just too stubborn to admit that I'm your mystery match, babe. It's up to me to make you see it."

"You're not right for me," I replied, "and this stunt today proves it."

"But what about your fortune?" Jeremy challenged.

"Even if your face were to appear in a crystal ball right before my eyes, Jeremy, I would never take you back!"

I whirled around and marched back into the restaurant with Jeremy on my heels.

Mr. Romano was standing at the counter in back. "Jeremy, I'd like to speak to you in the kitchen, please." His voice was ominous, and the finger he crooked in Jeremy's direction looked larger than life.

Well, I thought glumly, *there was no point in leaving early now.*

I busied myself serving coffee to the secretaries. Before I knew it, Jeremy was weaving his way toward the entrance.

"I hope you're satisfied," he hissed in my ear. "I lost my job."

"You blew it all on your own," I replied, holding my chin up bravely. "It's about time you stop blaming other people for your problems. Just face up to your mistakes for once."

"You'll be sorry you turned me down," he predicted, pulling open the glass door. "Plenty of girls at school like me just the way I am."

"Plenty of girls would love to date you," I agreed in all honesty. But I was simply no longer one of them.

Chapter Ten

I was too keyed up to sleep that night. For hours I tossed and turned, playing back Jeremy's dirty trick over and over again in my mind. I was angry at him for tampering with the clock and angry with myself for not catching on to his scheme. I should have been more alert to his guilty expression when I caught him folding up the step stool after lunch. I should have checked my watch. I should have realized that the clock *had* to be off, that time couldn't have been moving that slowly. But it was too late to make the driver's exam appointment. Too late to meet Mark as we'd planned.

The worst part of the entire mess was that Mark was mad at me. Furious, to be exact. It had been years since he'd really lit into me the way he had today. Even though I hadn't been able to see his face today over the telephone, I could easily imagine the fury in his gray eyes and the determined set of his square chin.

Of course the situation was entirely different than what he thought. I wasn't at fault, Jeremy was! I would have to set the record straight with Mark first thing in the morning, I decided, giving my pillow a determined punch.

"But Mark isn't here," Mandy said through the Bennetts' back screen door the following morning.

"It's only nine o'clock," I protested, following her into the country-style kitchen that's almost identical to ours.

Mandy was still dressed in her pink nightie. She padded across the linoleum to pour herself a glass of orange juice at the counter. "Mark and Peter went to work at the crack of dawn to help Sid with inventory. I guess they like to do that stuff before store hours."

"Oh." I stuffed my hands in the pockets of my red shorts and paced back and forth across the floor. "I was too wrapped up in my problems to even notice that Peter was gone."

"Want some juice?" Mandy asked.

"No thanks," I replied, continuing to pace the floor.

"Mark told me what happened," Mandy said, looking confused. "It's not like you to lose track of time, Karen. Taking the test seemed so important to you."

"It *was* important!" Then I told her what Jeremy had done.

"That—that *monster*! I hope you've crossed him off your list for good!" Mandy fumed.

"I'm definitely through with him!" I said. "He's still too selfish to let me run my own life. Having my independence has never been more important to me than it is now. Handling the job at the Nook has made me all the more self-sufficient." I paused for a moment. "As a matter of fact, I've decided to give up my search for my mystery match as well," I said.

"No!" Mandy gasped. "You can't just throw away a fortune. Anything that shows up in a crystal ball is—well—official." Mandy looked around the room as if she expected a sign to appear somewhere.

I shook my head. "This has gotten to be a big waste of time. It's not worth the aggravation. Besides, who's to know if that fortune-teller was even for real?"

"Well, we have to fix your love life up somehow . . ." Mandy bit determinedly into a sugared doughnut.

"I've decided to just sit back and let love happen," I said. "Chasing around town in search of some secret love hasn't gotten me anywhere."

"But—"

"If you really want to help, Mandy, come with me to Sid's Liquidators this morning. I want to clear things up with Mark, and I'd really appreciate your support."

"But we'd have to take the bus down to the business district," Mandy moaned. "And that's such a pain. Can't you call him on the phone?"

"No, I want to talk to him face to face," I insisted.

Mandy nodded reluctantly. "Okay—I understand. Maybe Mark will listen to you if he sees you face-to-face."

We got to Fairmont's business district about an hour later. It's a part of town that Mandy and I don't normally visit—it's on the outskirts of downtown and really has little to offer teenage girls. Warehouses and wholesale outlets line the streets for several blocks. There's not a clothing store, jewelry shop, or hamburger place in sight.

As we walked down a cracked concrete sidewalk toward Sid's Liquidators, we wondered why neither one of us had ever checked out the place where our brothers worked.

"We've mainly stayed away from Sid's because the guys told us to," I pointed out.

"True," Mandy agreed, moving behind me for a minute to let a group of men pass us by on the narrow walkway. "But let's face it. If they worked at the mall, they couldn't keep us away with a whip."

I laughed. "That's for sure!"

Unlike some of the storefronts we'd passed, Sid's front window was squeaky clean—so clean that the sun glistened on the glass as if it were polished crystal. And unlike some of the quiet warehouses nearby, Sid's was alive with activity.

The store was filled with customers and noise. Display models of various TV's and stereos were tuned into different channels, making a constant, garbled hum. Eight checkout lines moved steadily along, and the clerks behind the cash registers were hopping. Sid's was definitely a lot more interesting than our brothers had let on!

We roamed the aisles in search of Mark. Around us was everything from bicycles to washers to boom boxes, all on sale at rock-bottom prices, but I was too nervous to stop and browse.

"There he is," Mandy suddenly said, tugging at my sleeve. "Over there, in the computer stuff."

Mark was in the adjoining aisle, looking very professional in his gray pants, light blue shirt, and navy and gray striped tie. He was sifting through the contents of a huge cardboard box with a price gun in his hand, completely unaware that we were nearby.

We rounded the corner and stood behind him for a moment, watching him as he pulled packages of software out of the box, priced each one with a practiced stroke, and swung them onto their proper hooks.

Mandy cleared her throat. "Young man, where on earth can I find the heating pads?" she quavered like an old lady. "Slipshod place you have here! Nothing in order!"

Mark whirled around in surprise. He didn't smile when he saw who it was. "What are you doing here?" he demanded, pointing the price gun at us like a lethal weapon.

I stared at him, tongue-tied under his piercing glare.

But Mandy couldn't resist the chance to needle him. "Don't shoot! Don't shoot!" she pleaded.

"Mark, I have to talk to you about yesterday. I have to—" I stumbled over the words.

"Karen, I can't discuss it here," Mark cut in.

But I'd come too far to stop now. "Jeremy set the clock at the Nook back to stop me from meeting you," I explained in a rush. "He was trying to run my life again, the way he did while I was dating him."

Mark stared at me. "Really?" he said. "What a jerk. What did you do about it?"

"I told him that his little trick had completely ruined things for him—that I didn't want to see him *ever* again," I replied, and suddenly Mark looked much happier. "Mr. Romano was pretty upset, too. He fired Jeremy on the spot."

"Great," Mark said, his face glowing with satisfaction. "That jerk deserved it."

"What are you girls doing here?" a familiar voice demanded behind us. I turned to see my brother marching toward us.

"We came to see *Mark*," I replied, irritated. Peter sounded as bossy as ever.

"So you saw him. Now get out of here and let us do our jobs," Peter commanded, pointing in the direction of the front door.

I was about to protest his orders when a voice on the store's intercom system interrupted. "Tom Bedford, line one. Tom Bedford, line one."

The low, husky voice was familiar somehow. "Who's that?" I asked.

"Tom Bedford is a college guy that works here," Mark answered quickly, bending over his box of software again.

"No, no," I objected. "The woman. The voice on the speaker."

Peter and Mark glanced at each other. "I don't have time for this game," Peter said sharply, trying to propel us toward the door. "That was Sid on the speaker."

"But Sid is a man," Mandy protested, not moving an inch. "That sounded like a woman."

"Sid is a woman," Mark said flatly. "Her real name is Louise Sidney. Everybody calls her Sid."

"Yeah," Peter agreed. "No big deal. Goodbye."

The intercom crackled once more as if another announcement was about to follow. Peter tried to push us along, but I stood my ground, intent on listening. "Watch for the flashing-light special in our small appliance department. Blenders, coffee makers at our lowest prices for the next ten minutes. Prices will never be lower in the future. . . ."

In the future . . . There was something about the way Sid had said the word "future." Suddenly it hit me. Sid was Xaviera!

"What's wrong?" Mandy asked me. "You look sort of funny."

"My head is spinning, that's all," I said coldly, looking from Peter to Mark.

"What's wrong, kid?" Peter asked. He sounded offhand, but I knew him too well. He was nervous about something.

"You know what's wrong," I said indignantly. "Sid is Xaviera! No wonder you guys plotted to keep me away from here. You conned me all the way. You hired her to feed me a phony fortune just to steer me away from Jeremy, didn't you?"

"Yeah, kind of," Peter admitted, busily adjusting his tie to avoid meeting my gaze. He looked as if he was on the verge of laughter and was trying to conceal it. "Look, Mark and I just couldn't stand by and let you mope your life away. We knew how hung up you are on mysterious things, so we decided to spark the adventurous side of you—get you back into circulation.

What better way than to send you off in search of Mr. Right?" Peter shook his head with a grin. "Boy, did it ever work. You fell for it like a ton of bricks."

"When we caught Mark in the alley at the party, he'd really just taken Xaviera home, hadn't he?" I turned from Peter to get the answer from Mark.

"Yes," Mark admitted uncomfortably, running a finger under his collar.

"And Peter must've returned the earring to Xaviera," Mandy said slowly.

Peter nodded with a wide smile, even though I was glaring at him.

"I suppose you even told her what to say," I said coldly.

"I wrote her a note," Peter replied, trying to stifle his laughter. "But she couldn't have used many of my suggestions. You sure haven't turned into the devoted sister I said she should tell you to be."

"She was a phony!" I cried, totally humiliated. "Nothing but a fraud!"

Peter must finally have realized how hard I was taking all of this. He stopped laughing and spoke in a gentler tone. "You were so down about being without a boyfriend that we wanted to help you snap out of it. When Mom came up with the fortune teller routine, it seemed like the perfect opportunity to add some spice to your life.

"You should give me some credit," he continued. "It took a lot of planning and expert timing. I hid Mom's fishbowl right before the party and sent her off on a wild goose chase to buy another one. In the meantime, Mark picked up Sid at her house and slipped her into the garage through the alley. After she told your fortune, Mark whisked her away again—only minutes before Mom was ready to tell your fortune."

"I can't believe you'd do that to me!" I snapped.

"Please don't be mad, Karen," Mark said. He looked worried.

"The two of you make a fool of me in front of the whole town of Fairmont and I shouldn't be mad?" Tears were burning the rims of my eyes, but I held them back. I had that much pride left. "Let's go, Mandy," I said, tugging at her arm. Mandy flashed the two guys an angry look and followed me out the door.

We were silent on the bus ride home. I stared out the window at the scenery, not really seeing any of it. I was too wrapped up in my thoughts and too busy dwelling on the embarrassing things I'd done. I had made a tremendous project out of the search for my love match while those two jerks stood on the sidelines, watching and laughing at my every move.

How could I ever face Mark again? I wondered. I could handle Peter. He was a dumb brother who had done plenty of stupid things himself, like taping his ears back so they wouldn't stick out when he was little.

But Mark was—well, a regular guy. A guy who had been acting a whole lot less like a second pesky brother lately. It was disappointing to learn that he'd taken a step backward by participating in Peter's dumb "brainstorm."

"Want to come over for a soda or something?" I asked Mandy as the bus stopped at our street corner.

"Sure," Mandy said with a grimace. "Maybe we can think of some horrible revenge!"

A short time later Mandy and I were seated on my living room sofa, feet propped up on the coffee table, griping.

"I go to all the trouble of taking two buses down to the business district to apologize to Mark, only to end up looking like a clown," I said.

"Bus ride to humiliation," Mandy stated grimly. "Sounds almost like a movie title, doesn't it?"

"A low-budget movie, maybe," I replied with a groan.

Suddenly the doorbell rang. "I wonder who that could be?" I set my drink down on the table and headed for the front door.

"Maybe it's the boy of your dreams," Mandy suggested.

"It's probably the boy collecting for the news-paper," I said dryly.

I swung open the door to find the last person on earth I expected to see.

"It's you!" I exclaimed, taking a step backward.

"May I come in?" the low, husky voice asked.

Awestruck, I stared into Xaviera's dark eyes. I nodded and stepped aside so she could walk in.

Chapter Eleven

"So, we meet again," Xaviera said huskily, her dark eyes pinning me to the wall just as surely as if she had pushed me up against it.

"Would you—would you like to talk in the living room?" I asked nervously. Mandy was staring at us, stunned.

"Yes. I would like that very much," she replied.

"Please sit down." I trailed behind my strange guest. Even out of her gypsy garb, she had a mystical aura. Her gray hair was wound in a knot at the base of her neck. Her clothes—though a far cry from her colorful costume—still looked exotic. Her maroon blouse billowed around her slender frame, and the hem of her black skirt floated around her ankles as if it were lighter than air.

"There is trouble, Karen Daly," she stated solemnly, dropping onto the sofa beside Mandy. If

142

I hadn't been so shocked by Xaviera's sudden entrance, I would have laughed over Mandy's discomfort. My friend had begun to slowly edge her way to the far side of the sofa, her mouth hanging open. It took a lot to make Mandy that nervous.

"There *is* trouble," I repeated sarcastically.

"You doubt my authenticity. Is that correct?" she inquired briskly. Her eyes never left me as I sank down on a chair across the room.

"Well, yes . . ." I trailed off, tongue-tied.

"Did you read her mind with your powers?" Mandy asked hoarsely, her eyes wide.

"No, young lady, those words rang out very clearly through my store. They penetrated my ears without any mystical aid whatsoever."

"I'm sorry," I said. "But I caught Peter and Mark red-handed. They hired you to con me with a fake fortune."

"They hired me with that intention," Xaviera admitted, nodding slowly. "But," she said, shaking a ringed finger at me, "I gave you a genuine reading." She chuckled half to herself. "They got much more than they bargained for, those rambunctious young fellows."

"I still stand by my predictions," Xaviera declared, her dark eyes shining like black marbles. She opened the gold bag in her lap and removed two envelopes. "Here you are, Karen," she said, thrusting the envelopes in my direction. "These are the instructions from Peter and Mark. As you see, they are still sealed." She smiled widely, looking highly amused. "I do not need two little boys to advise me on such matters. I have been at it for a long, long time."

I leaned forward and accepted the two envelopes. Both were pieces of Sid's Liquidators stationery, and both had 'SID' scrawled on the front.

"Where did you get the name Xaviera?" Mandy asked. I had wondered if her natural inquisitiveness would overcome her nerves.

"My husband and I owned a traveling carnival for many years. I told fortunes in a small trailer, and Xaviera was my professional name. I tired of the travel after my husband died, and decided to sell the carnival and invest the money in another business. That is how Sid's Liquidators came to be."

"Wow," Mandy gasped. "Will you tell *my* fortune sometime?"

"Sometime," Xaviera agreed, rising to her feet. "I must go now. There is work to be done at the store."

"Thank you for these," I said, holding up the envelopes. "And for coming to explain things."

Xaviera paused at the front door. "Good luck, Karen. May you enjoy all the future holds for you."

The moment the front door closed behind

Xaviera, Mandy was on her feet, grabbing at the envelopes. "Let's open these and see what those rats were trying to pull."

I handed one to Mandy and opened the other. Mine was obviously written in Peter's loose scrawl. "Listen to this, Mandy," I said in a dry tone. " 'Tell my sister to get on with the program and forget about Jeremy Miller. If she disagrees (which she's in the habit of doing) lay it on really thick about some mystery boy being in love with her. Tell her to search all over town for him if she has to. That should keep her busy this summer! Also mention that she should be kinder to her brother. Tell her that I'm going to be a famous movie director some day and she might want to iron my shirts for half price and make my bed from time to time to stay in good with me. Promise her a big part in my first flick if she behaves herself!' "

Mandy broke up completely. "That's Peter for you! Always trying to arrange things."

"Read Mark's," I instructed.

"Okay," Mandy said, ripping open the envelope. "Let's see."

As she scanned the letter, her laughter stopped and her face suddenly became very sober.

"What does it say?" I asked impatiently, trying to reach for the paper.

"I'll read it to you," Mandy said, pulling it out of my reach. "But I don't believe it."

145

"Mandy!" I coaxed. "C'mon."

"All right. 'Dear Sid: Rip up Peter's letter. Karen deserves much better than that. The mystery match idea is fine. But be sure not to lead her all over town looking for love. Tell her that love is right next door.'"

Mandy stopped to stare at me. "Wow! Who would have ever guessed that it was my dumb brother!"

I dropped onto the sofa. So it was Mark all the time! My thoughts drifted back to our encounter on the beach. I was sure that if we'd kissed that night, no gypsy would have been needed as a go-between.

Mandy looked sheepish. "I'm sorry, Karen. I guess you feel a little disappointed, huh?"

"No!" I said quickly. "But I am surprised. I should have realized something was up during the party when we discovered him in the alley. He was so interested in my fortune, remember?"

"He should've just told you the truth," Mandy said.

"He couldn't," I pointed out. I took the letter and glanced over it. "The four of us have been pals for too long to blurt out something like that. If I'd rejected him, he would have been so humiliated. And Peter would've mocked him about it all the time. Mark doesn't even want Peter to know he's thinking of being a teacher.

146

He thinks it sounds too dull for my colorful brother."

"So he was using Xaviera to deliver his message," Mandy said thoughtfully. "That way, you could ignore it completely if you wanted to."

"And save our friendship, I suppose."

"How *do* you feel about Mark?" Mandy asked curiously.

"I—I don't know. I have to sort this out," I replied. It seemed only right to talk to Mark first, before I shared my feelings with Mandy. Besides, this love angle to our friendship was going to take a little getting used to!

I spent the rest of the afternoon shut away in my room, deep in thought. Thinking of Mark as a boyfriend wasn't hard to do at all. He was one of the nicest boys I'd ever known.

But how could I reach him, after all that had happened during the last couple of days? First he'd been angry with me about missing the driver's exam. Then I'd blown up at him about hiring Xaviera. We had been so busy shouting at each other that it didn't seem right to just pop next door to say hello!

An idea finally occurred to me about seven o'clock that evening. And luck was with me—Peter was at a baseball game with a date and Mandy was shopping with her mother. Both of them were too far away to poke their noses into my plan. If Mark and I were going to settle things, it had to be on a one-to-one basis, not with the usual foursome. I picked up the telephone and dialed Romano's Pizza Nook with a very special request. Luckily, Maria answered the phone, and was eager to help me.

The clock on the kitchen wall read eight o'clock as I reached into the refrigerator for a can of soda. Where was he? I wondered with a sinking feeling in my heart. Maybe it was all too much for him. I sat down at the table and opened the can. Maybe he had decided to give up on me. In a way I couldn't blame him, but in a way I was ready to strangle him. Now I knew how he must have felt watching me bumble around looking for my match. I would just have to wait and hope something wonderful would happen.

I sat in the kitchen for a while, listening to the radio and sipping on my cola.

"Pizza anyone?"

Mark's friendly face was peeking through the screen door. "Come in," I invited nervously as a wave of shyness swept over me.

The screen door creaked and Mark stepped inside. He looked wonderful in a royal blue polo shirt and red shorts. His curly black hair looked freshly shampooed, and his gray eyes held a familiar twinkle. "Hi. I just wondered if you'd like to share this Romano's special that was mysteriously delivered to my door," he said, setting the pizza box on the table. "Still piping hot from the oven."

"Great. Sit down and I'll get you some soda," I said. I headed for the refrigerator, hoping he wouldn't notice how wobbly my knees were. "You, uh, look at the pizza yet?" I asked, concentrating on the contents of the refrigerator.

"I sure did," he murmured in my ear. I jumped a little. He was standing right behind me all of a sudden, his hands resting on my shoulders.

Mark gently turned me toward him and cupped my chin in his hand. He stood only a few inches taller than me, so I had no choice but to look him in the eye.

"Orange or cola?" I asked, my voice sounding a bit off-key.

"That can wait," he whispered. His gray eyes were sparkling silver, and a smile was forming on his lips.

He was going to kiss me. And this time I knew it wasn't an impulse sparked by a romantic bonfire—or a fortune-teller. This time it was for real.

Then it happened. Mark's lips were on mine, warm and soft. My pulse hammered as I placed my hands on his chest. I closed my eyes and inhaled his woodsy after-shave thinking about how great it smelled at such close range.

"I'm glad you finally figured out it was me," Mark said gently after our kiss.

"It would have saved me a lot of investigative work if I had done it sooner," I said with a laugh. "But Xaviera threw things out of whack when she gave me a genuine, more cryptic fortune."

"Yeah, she told me the truth the day after the party," Mark said with a frown. "She was pretty amused by her trick, but I was devastated. It seemed like my only shot at letting you know how I felt."

"I understand why you did it that way," I said, toying with the knit collar of his shirt. "Our whole friendship could've blown up in our faces if you'd just hollered your feelings over the back fence."

"Maybe I just should have," Mark chuckled. "Peter's shocked expression would have been priceless."

"I think you handled everything very well," I assured him. "The four of us have been friends for years, and you tried to protect our friendship. That was really thoughtful of you."

"I suppose you were pretty surprised to discover it was me," Mark said with a sheepish smile.

"Yes," I admitted. "But maybe I shouldn't have been. Our relationship has been growing over the past year. I've noticed different things in you lately, especially since our lessons began."

"I began to notice you as a regular girl when you started dating Jeremy."

"A regular girl?" I objected. "I've always been one of those!"

"Not to me," Mark explained. "You were always the kid next door—Mandy's little pal. Then all of a sudden you were wearing makeup and going out on dates. I fell so hard for you. And it was awful watching you go steady with that jerk."

"Well, I guess we have a head start on other couples," I said. "We're already the best of friends."

"And we already trust each other," Mark added. "You know, this seems like the perfect time to officially end the search for your mystery match."

"The search is officially over," I whispered as he leaned forward once more to kiss me. I kept my eyes open for a second and saw the open pizza box on the table over his shoulder with the heart-shaped pizza inside. Being so deeply involved in the pizza business, I hadn't been able to think of a better way to get my romantic message across.

"We seem to be standing in a draft," Mark commented, pushing the refrigerator shut behind me.

"I guess I didn't notice," I giggled. "Let's sit down and have our pizza now. And discuss when I'm going to take my driver's exam."

"It feels good to be alone together for a change," Mark said, settling back in one of the oak chairs.

It *was* a nice change, but we weren't alone for long. Peter barged through the back door just as I finished slicing up the sausage and pepperoni heart. "Hey, check out that crazy pizza!" he exclaimed.

"Mr. Romano went overboard with ingredients," I observed. "It has at least twice the normal amount of toppings."

"Looks like an Italian valentine." Peter sniffed the air appreciatively and dropped down into a chair with a thud.

"Want to join us?" I invited with mild sarcasm.

"Don't you want me?" Peter glanced at Mark with a pitiful expression.

"Looks as if we're stuck with you," Mark surrendered, slapping my brother on the back. "Just like always."

Peter shook his head in confusion. "I feel like I've missed something. You know, like when you start watching your favorite TV show after the first commercial break. You recognize everybody, but they've already started something up and you can't quite tune into it."

Mark and I exchanged a glance and concentrated on the pizza. I couldn't help smiling.

"Why do I get the feeling that love is in the air?" Peter asked suspiciously.

"We might as well set the record straight," I said with a grin. "You guessed right."

"Really?" Peter questioned. "That's great!"

I turned to stare at him in shock. Was this really *Peter* talking? "Aren't you going to needle us?" Mark demanded in a shocked tone. "Aren't you going to ask how I could feel romantic about your kid sister?"

Peter laughed shortly, raising a palm in self-defense. "I know where you're coming from. A couple of weeks ago, I would've laughed you out of town. But after teaching Mandy to drive . . . Well, I've learned that things can get pretty tangled up between even the oldest of friends."

"Been feeling tangled up lately?" I probed with a teasing grin.

"Yeah," Peter confessed, blowing out a lungful of air. "I've been tangled up in wide eyes, excited chatter, and lots of pink bubble gum!"

"Are you telling us you're in love with Mandy?" I asked excitedly. This was just too much!

"Cool your jets, kid," Peter said, rubbing the back of his neck nervously. "I'm only saying that I understand how unpredictable life can be. I'm used to dating quiet girls who let me tell the jokes and steer the car. But—"

"Are you having a party in there?" Mandy opened the door and marched in with a hurt expression. "I heard your voices from the house

153

and thought I'd investigate." She sat down beside Peter. "Hey, look at that crazy pizza!"

"Help yourself," I invited with a sigh.

"You should be home asleep, Mandy," Peter complained. "You want to be fresh for your driver's exam tomorrow."

"Who died and left you boss?" Mandy shot back.

"I just want you to pass the first time so I'm off the hook," Peter retorted.

"Well, if I flunk, it's because of your inferior lessons," Mandy said.

Mark leaned over and took my chin in his hand.

"Now?" I murmured, realizing that he was about to kiss me right then and there in the midst of the heated battle.

"I think we'd better get used to them," he advised ruefully as he gave me a gentle kiss. "They come with the territory."